# God Head

Library of Congress Cataloging-in-Publication Data
Zwiren, Scott, 1964-
    God head / Scott Zwiren.
        p.    cm.
    I. Title.
PS3576.W47G63        1996        813'.54—dc20        96-7375
ISBN 1-56478-130-5


                    Dalkey Archive Press
                    Illinois State University
                    Campus Box 4241
                    Normal, IL 61790-4241

*Printed on permanent/durable acid-free paper and bound in the
United States of America*

**Scott Zwiren**

# GOD HEAD

**Dalkey Archive Press**

## SUMMER 1991

I am waiting to know what I am because I don't know.
For the past few days I've known I have become something else, or am in the process of becoming something
else. Maybe something good, maybe something bad.
Maybe something very good. Maybe something incredibly bad. Maybe both.

I'm waiting for a sign. It could be simple. I flick an ash
onto the table and brush it off with my hand. "Ah, you're
an angel," I think to myself, and there's something
about that thought that resonates above the others.
Then it hits me. It hits me like a bolt of the rawest
light—like a revelation worth waiting a lifetime for—I am
an angel. That's what I am becoming. I'm becoming an
angel without dying. It's very uncomfortable, very uncomfortable. I feel it pop inside me, all over, pop! pop!
pop!—like my head's expanding, no, burning. I've been
sitting on it for days like a headache and now the realization of it is an assault.

I jump up overwhelmed, I've got to get out. I've got to
walk off my head; all that material world matter is peeling away too fast. I've got to get outside and walk. I can
hear pauses between the words and the letters in the
thoughts in my head and I know I have to enjoy it or it'll
hurt. Then, bang, the door closes behind me and the

elevator opens, but when I get in this space it's even smaller than the hall, and I'm going to be in it for a long, long, long time.

Loud and echoing, faster and faster, I'm running because I'm going to expand: taking everything, everything with me.

Once I knew I was an angel meant to save. But it's changed: I know it is myself that everything else must be saved from. I must be the Exterminating Angel. When I spread my wings—BANG!

This must be an initiation.

The door waves open and I'm sucked out, almost flying out on to the street . . . a tree, 54 W 105 St, a streetlight, a car . . . it's all going by me . . . 56 W 105 St, another tree, a car, 58 W 105 St, garbage pails, another tree, a car, a car, a car, a car, but I'll never reach the corner. I'll never get there and I'll explode so violently that the shock waves will cover the world, spreading out from 105 St like a fan of destruction, sucking everything into the vortex, and the only reason this doesn't happen is because the addresses jump numbers, putting me safely on the corner, so I keep walking past there until I'm sure everything is OK, and even then, I keep going, because I can't stop—the bodega, the sandwich shop, the liquor store, the travel agency, the beauty salon . . . CHECKS CASHED . . . SUPERMARKET . . . TOBACCO SHOP . . . COFFEE SHOP . . . DON'T WALK! I can't wait for the light and so I'm crossing wherever the light's with me and I keep walking, I reach a corner and then I cross at the green light, following the green light no matter where it takes me, 73 W 106 St, a tree, a car, a garbage pail, 75 W 106 St, a car, a tree, a garbage pail, 77 W 106 St, a tree, a car, a pail . . . until I reach the corner . . . DON'T WALK . . . PIZZA . . . SUPERMARKET . . . TOBACCO SHOP . . . and when it says

WALK I keep walking and when it's red . . . CHECKS CASHED
. . . COFFEE SHOP . . . and says DON'T WALK, I'm going with
the green . . . 93 W 106 St, A TREE . . . A CAR . . . A GARBAGE
PAIL . . . chasing the green light, 97 W 106 St, A TREE, A
TREE, A GARBAGE PAIL . . . there's no red light I can wait for,
100 W 106 St . . . A CAR, A CAR, A STREETLIGHT . . . no place
to be but following the green lights. I will never be able
to wait in front of a stoplight ever.

Wherever I go the light's with me. I can't stand still
long enough to wait for a light to change.

I see a man in a blue shirt going Uptown.

It asks me—Blue up? and because I almost did blow
up I know I have to follow him up Amsterdam Avenue
until I come to a dead stop in front of the Hungarian
Pastry Shop.

Drawing me in, for a purpose I'll find inside, where
it's not a moment before I realize, Can I help you? They
expect me to order. It's part of the front. I say, A coffee.
She asks for my name, and when they have your name
they have everything. They might as well have your
soul. In the dimly lit café I can see, under the small
lamps along the wall, ghostly men and women, looking
academic, all completely robbed of their souls, and I ask
her why she wants my name. She says they call out
your name and bring you your coffee, and I say that I'll
take my own coffee.

She is really insulted, afraid of letting one soul slip
through. She looks almost hurt and confused and I am
sad that, being almost an angel, I am higher than she is.

Now I know why I'm where I am, on the street across
from Saint John's Cathedral, next door to Saint Luke's
Hospital, so close to the saints, drinking coffee with the
ghosts, and knowing it isn't enough just to cross over
to the saints, but on what corner, going which way.

Reaching into my pocket knowing it never fails me and pulling out a flat soft pack with one flat cigarette and a lighter, a good green one, most importantly in that order, the order of things always important, and blowing halos of smoke, to hail an angel, they're attracted to halos like people to hellos and they come like cabs.

It's not long before a man sits down beside me, and I'm sure we're both tourists on the material plane traveling incognito on the wrong side of the street, where if the hungry ghosts knew what we were they'd eat us like pastry, like the Hungarian pastry under the counter.

I can't say anything that will give us away, seem incredible or unnatural, and phrased just so that the instruction I need is included but general enough not to draw attention to us. I ask him where Saint John's is and he looks up from his book and smiles and says that it is right across the street.

He gives it the thumbs up and goes back to reading.

So I pay for my coffee, walking out the door to my right, the cathedral is on the left, but I go right and make a right at the corner, keep making rights until I'm around the block and in front of the cathedral, always going right because the directions were *right* across the street, and you always follow the directions exactly because it's not where you arrive but how you arrive there that makes all the difference.

The thumbs up—that refers to my coronation.

At the top of the stairs is an arch, Christ sitting majestically underneath, suspended in a circle that floats over the heads of personalities from the Bible, both testaments, some still uncarved, and a sign beneath that says Carvings in the Portals of Paradise.

You can't get in that way. It's unfinished, but I look around and see people entering at a side door. Without a plan now, assuming that looking and finding was the way all this time, I realize that my reward is looking for me. In the Fountain of Peace, attracted to it and attracting it, *right* across the street, next to the cathedral and right across the street from the terminal of ghosts, I stop moving. For the first time since the world was saved on my street corner, a long time ago, I stop and read the plaque on the sculpture which describes the rescue of heaven, threatened by Satan, by the archangel Michael on a pedestal. All of it is passing into me as I am losing my sense of differences and time and memory in the sacrifice for wings. The connections whiz by from the pastry shop to paradise to peace. The triangle. It leads me astray but right on the path so I'll be in the right location at the right time, *right* across the street where angels, all around the world, sit outside a cathedral to be rung into being by cathedral bells. All of it coming together faster and faster. When an ambulance siren comes down Amsterdam Avenue I think, You've been coronated.

The worst is over now, no more uncertainty, there's no panic because I am what I will be and wherever I am I'm there at the right time provided I follow the signs. Learning to be a good citizen crossing at the green and stopping at the red, it is always as simple as that. I'm going back to my room by the shortest route knowing exactly how to cross the street.

I see a woman with two dogs. She's waiting for the light to change. We acknowledge each other, and everything goes dark except her eyes. She claims me in the friendliest way. She passes and the world goes on again. I AM HIM, I AM HE, I AM, I AM, I AM, now the woman with the dogs has identified me but instead of saying Christ, I know to tell the door intercom of the residence the name they know me by and they let me in like it is any other day.

Fumbling with the keys, in through the door, falling to the bed in the bedroom with the doors closed and windows shut, I scream I AM! The tears coming down my face, remembering every time they put me in the hospital when they didn't understand, when I was naive enough to tell them who I really am, my mother pleading for me not to say it anymore. Every collapse was just a prelude, getting ready, changing, taking leaps, preparing for right now.

Except that I belong to someone now, which doesn't belong, I belong to all, but I belong to her, the woman on the corner who claimed me, and I belong to her over them, and if I am Christ and he is absolute, none greater than, then she can't be or I am not him, that she is he, and not me, and everything comes out from under, and nothing stops me from falling through the black under my eyelids. I ask someone to save me, to show me, someone who loves me, and like a bullet of light with a cap her face coming at me I have to open my eyes to stop it. I am her reaching me from somewhere near, around the corner, and saying she loves me and being loved I feel good again knowing there is good and not evil in her long swishing skirt, earth colored, and of nature, and her hypnotic glance of white magic and its friendly persuasion. Could it be our union is the Messiah, and there is a duality in it, that it is part of my rite to serve her, that there is a community of messiahs each with his own territory, I and she being the West Side Messiah whose job is just to save our turf, getting involved with building, housing, crime, drugs, and parks? I see how the prophecy will happen. Finding my new text, retaining messiahship, I am glad, but important new questions arise, like why am I in bed and the answer is because this is the night of my consummation and there's no need to find her, she will come here, she will know everything, she will take me to a new life, except she can't walk through doors.

I get up and go to the living room and unlock the door. Now there are preparations—whatever I'll need will be ready for me, like the garlic on the table from the pizza last night, which I dumped on the floor in a circle, and the matches I burned in a hat, and the paintings I turned upside down, and the painting I started and finished with a few strokes.

Now, needing some air, I'm on the stoop, leaving my keys in the house and locking the door as a sign of leaving my old life, meeting her halfway as a gesture of sharing, waiting for her to come around the corner walking her dog, and waiting and waiting, noticing that every move I make has a simultaneous answer around me—I stamp my foot, the light changes; I turn my head, a car stops abruptly—and I'm not grandiose in each power because it's not me making it happen, but me happening with it and I know that if I see her at the coffee shop and across from my building, and at Columbus and 105th and in the square where she walks her dogs, then it only leaves 106th and Manhattan, across from the church with the big cross, I'm sitting on a pump waiting for her to come walking her dog at midnight and me joining them, a Saint Bernard I'd be if I were a dog and the command is stay, and I notice that a lot of other women are walking dogs, they must be witches, witches who are designated by the color they wear, and I'm wearing lavender and white, which means that my top half is of the highest rank and my bottom half is in the spiritual realm, all of them walking around toward midnight on the night when the witches show their colors.

A guy stands on the corner in a black and red striped shirt, a courier, a woman gets out of a taxi wearing lavender and white and I stare her down, and she stares at me and walks by, and I follow the colors and configurations waiting, waiting.

Then a man comes up to me and smiles, and he asks me if I am wearing shorts and I say I'm not, I haven't worn underwear for days since I ran out of them. He asks if I want to split one. So I say not with him, knowing what he means, and trying to push him off. He looks hurt and asks, Why not, and unable to explain the whole thing I ask how big this territory is, wondering if it belonged to the witches or the messiahs. And he doesn't know what I'm talking about. I was just let in on it today and he obviously is still in the dark. But he offers me a beer and I say I have to stay here—holding up the building, on a johnny pump pedestal, Angel, Messiah, and Saint Bernard, I retain all identities, even my own name. So he goes and I'm waiting and waiting when along comes a man and woman who are definitely insiders. She looks at me in a funny way like she knows, and when he comes out again I ask him what time it is and he says one o'clock, so I don't know what to do now, the woman who claimed me didn't walk her dog at midnight and maybe it is all a mistake.

The witches run the city. They ride in the ambulances like the ambulances are a private limousine service. I see a crack addict dressed all in white stop an ambulance at a red light and conduct it on its way. Observation. Inference. Conclusion.

Since no woman walked her dog at midnight, I'm coming back to reality, that I am the one and only Him and there is no community of me, just me, and until there is a formal brotherhood of man I will be lonely with the burden of being the chosen.

I'm back sitting on my residence stoop when this girl sits down next to me. She says her name and I tell her right out that I think I'm Christ. She asks me how old I am. I say twenty-six. She says not to worry, that I got seven good years left. She asks for a quarter and I reach in the pocket of infinite change and pull out a dime, a nickel, another dime, another nickel, and a penny. The miracle is beginning so long as I hold onto the multiplying and others gathering around to witness the miracle and it's decided how we can get a beer, a bottle of wine from the black market seller down the street, and a bag of chips. All by gathering our resources while my community box of cigarettes is out for anyone to pick from. A dime gets one loose at the corner and if the pocket of infinite change is down for a minute there's always my wallet. We take the chips and beer and recite poetry on the bench in the park a block down. This is the new life, in the night hours when the cops come round less frequently. Later I go back in having been out all night and wait for the sun to come up at Harry's apartment and go to the community room and tell the other guys in the residence. I tell them that when light hits the street they all scatter, and they say I'm the man for the prostitutes on the block, and they won't leave me alone now that they know me and take all my money.

I go out again and then I decide it is time to go back in and press the buzzer and say the name they know for the intercom. I know that Harry's up so I go to his apartment, knock on the door, and he lets me in on that name but I tell him as soon as I get in that I'm Christ himself.

He checks the Hebrew calendar outside the kitchen and doesn't understand why it isn't sunrise yet. It's seven o'clock by now and there should be coffee in the community room downstairs. So I go down and huddle at the coffee urn waiting for the light to go on like we are in a monastery and it is morning sacrament.

The guys say that it's good I'm locked out of my place because I'd start pulling the TV out and all the furniture and all my money, because it's like that.

This morning I'm sitting on the porch imagining I am back on the cross when I first was Christ in the first coming, then I lay in bed with the radio blasting and every song is a love song and all of them directed at me. One of the guys brings me in a cup of coffee, my door left open, and I scream when I take it, my hands so incredibly sensitive. The residence manager comes in and asks me if I want to go to the hospital. I say yes. I'm sure to meet my destiny there. In the ambulance they ask me questions about my material identity, a strain to remember, and as we go through the streets siren off I know that this is my day of ascension. In the emergency room there are so many people waiting, all have been sent to protect, to see, and in the psych ER I've been waiting a long time, but it's OK and I see the eye, blue eye in the TV screen of the outside waiting room monitor. I'm waiting to be sent upstairs. They interview me and I don't talk about my coronation at all but stick to a language they understand. I say that I'm manic, and I think I'm God.

Having the presence of mind to know "I think I'm God" instead of "I am God," and especially to say "I'm manic" makes my admission debatable. The hospital is overcrowded and it may mean I'm coherent enough to go home. I always become perilously coherent in a small room before inquiring psychiatrists. Sitting in front of them I become my own worst advocate and they're ready to release me.

I don't know where I should be.

They decide to put me up for the night in the ER, up the whole night watching the march of evolution on the walls: At the top the eye and at the bottom the spiders and angels became demons and I turn away from them, shadow figures on the wall. I close my eyes to shut them out and it is brighter under there and patterns entertain me all night. Then there is the image of a man as if in a rearview mirror: he's blond and wearing sunglasses, I see him, and then a minute later a woman comes in the ER and she's very out of it, and behind her is that man.

I really need a cigarette. Everyone wants cigarettes in the ER.

The doctor from the next shift is in the doorway. I ask him if he knows what runs the ambulances and he shakes his head. I want to say witches but I say gasoline. I ask him why I can read his mind. He pauses and then says because I can, and that he is open to me. I am open to him.

I expect to be told that I am sick. The answer surprises me. It calms me. Is he being patronizing? Is he really saying that? The air is buzzing and I'm hallucinating under my eyelids and watching it like a picture show. I demand to know what I am. It comes back to the same question. Always the same question. That question. If I can read his mind, why am I asking him questions? Because it isn't a question, it is a test, a salutation, a password.

He says that they are going to try and slow me down.

## WINTER 1982

I want to go away. I don't want to be anywhere. Make the world disappear. I want to sleep and if I can't sleep, I will lie down with my eyes closed. I don't need the rest anymore, I just want to go. I can't concentrate and I have studies to do. There's a muting switch in my head that activates when I lie still with eyes closed, it dulls the pressure but it feels like wet cotton. I prefer wet cotton to the pressure, the hollow inside and pressure on the outside. Lying in the bottom bunk in my dorm room trying to study, reading the same page over and over again and not retaining it, finally realizing that studying is just something to do while I have to be conscious. I am using it as another muting switch. Look at the clock. Five o'clock. The window's black, so it's still night. My roommate is sleeping above me while I lie in bed wrapped in a fetal position around my psychology book. The print is filling my head but I'm not thinking about it. What am I thinking about? It hurts to think about what I am thinking about, and so I keep reading but it's like reading an eye chart. No meaning.

I stare at the wall.

Between classes I lie in bed and when I can no longer convince myself that I am trying to sleep I stare at the walls and then I have to be with someone, can't be alone, even if the dorm is almost empty and all that is left is someone I dislike. I knock on their door. I invent sentences if only to keep the guise that I have come to visit, to say something, when in fact that other person's presence is protecting me from something. It isn't loneliness, I am not lonely, it is a need for distraction, something to keep me from being in my skin.

But it's five o'clock in the morning and the only thing to protect me from my own skin is this textbook. I want to wake up my roommate, but what can I say? I want to talk? Fire! I want to say FIRE! because that's the only reason to wake someone up at five o'clock in the morning and then I want to talk but I don't have anything to talk about. I've talked to people during regular hours, friends who were students, students who were not really friends, and the campus counselor.

I sit across from her in her office and talk about the pros and cons of going home. She wants me to stay at school. She doesn't see the fire, and I can't tell her about it because it just comes out in a vacant stare, an inability to concentrate on school, on conversations, on her next question.

She says that I shouldn't worry. I'm suffering from a "post-admissions syndrome," I'm suffering from missing home, and it is natural and complicated by the fact that I have just turned seventeen and am young for college.

Look at the clock again. It's still five o'clock. It's also five o'clock back home. I speak to my mother on the phone. I call her and she says that she has talked to people about my situation. I say that I've talked to people about my situation too. I speak in brief sentences and let her do most of the talking. Sometimes I just hang on to the receiver and say nothing. I'm so frozen with panic that it comes out like I'm nonplussed. I can't explain how I feel or what's happening to me. I want to call now. But it's five o'clock in the morning. I want to call her and yell FIRE! into the receiver but that makes less sense than waking my roommate. I'm jealous of him. I'm jealous that he's sleeping and I've taken my allotment. I look back at the text, read a sentence, and look up. If only I could be like them, all of them, the rest of them, the students. They seem so at ease and so spontaneous. They fit together. That was the reason for meals, so everyone could join in and be like one another, do the same thing. It had nothing to do with hunger for me. I was eating but I wasn't hungry and I debated whether I should go down to meals at all, but if I didn't then I'd be in bed endlessly, because sometimes I don't go to classes either, and if I didn't go down to meals where I sat alone, then I'd be completely alone in the dorm, and I don't like that. My roommate is sleeping but he's undeniably there. His unconscious body is better than an empty room and an empty dorm when they all go down to meals.

It seems like a long time until breakfast and it is long both in distance and time. In order to get from my dorm to the dining hall I have to climb a hill. The Arts Building, a four-story building, is designed so that one can take the outside steps that lead up the hill and step off them onto its roof. During freshman week a bunch of us went on the roof. That was in September and now it is February right after the January session and the roof is white with snow. I haven't been on the roof since then, but I pass by it every time on my way to the dorm. I turn to it for a moment and then just keep going as though if I stood there looking at it, thinking about it, I would eventually have to walk to the edge, and at the edge, wait, getting up the nerve, how long would it take before I'd become an obvious beacon to the passersby below and they'd talk me down before the police and ambulance came? There is no fence or gate, it is just open, like poinsettias in a nursery. It says, We assume you all know how to treat heights so we afford you this view. Don't they know there are people who will misuse the Arts Building? Stop on the top step, no one coming and no one behind. The snow is falling so there aren't any crowds, there's a lot of snow on the ground, and it's a weekend. People who see you standing by the roof don't ask questions, don't even suspect, they just pass by and they don't know that you've been standing there for a half hour, forty-five minutes, an hour, transfixed, adrenaline pumping, wait . . . wait . . . and then now, walk to the edge, those ten yards over to the edge, and then the beauty of it is the people going up and down the stairs, they don't suspect a thing even now, a lot of people walk to the edge for the view and stand there. You're just watching the snow. It's only if someone is down there looking up and makes the connection that it could be over. They would say, Hey you!! What are you doing up there? How can I answer? Why am I up here? There's no good reason why I should be up here, nothing to commit suicide over except that all the things I've taken for granted, my ability to carry on a conversation, my ability to make a decision, my ability to sleep, to study, to laugh, to smile, and everything else that makes me *me* have left. One day I woke up someone else, it crept up, and so if I have to answer that question from the person at ground level, the most encompassing response I can give looking down is, I'm not myself.

Stare at the wall. Look at the clock. The minute hand has barely nudged off the twelve. Stare at the wall. At

the campus bookstore I look for the books for next
semester. I can't do this, I think to myself, and then I
put them back. I put them back in all their places and
then I walk out of the bookstore. The snow is coming
down and I think: I've got to do this. I've got to. What is
waiting for me at home? So I go back into the bookstore
and take each book back out and stand on line at the
register. It's a long line and it gives me enough time to
change my mind again and I go back to the bookshelves
and then I reverse again and head for the line and it
feels as if the commitment is a line for the slaughter.

Stare at the wall. Stare. I tell my mother when I speak
to her that I'm worried and I don't know why, and she
asks me if I want to come home. I say I don't know.
Going home would mean the end of the world, but staying, the world is collapsing all around me. The end is
near because at five o'clock while my mother is sleeping
and my roommate is sleeping and the cafeteria is three
hours from opening, there is a van on the road coming
to pick me up.

My censor is so strong that I can't write about it. Any
poetry I've been able to write in the past weeks has been
made up of clipped sentences. When I was interviewing
for the class I showed them to the instructor. I told him
I was unable to write a long sentence. He looked up at
me from the page, not seeming to process the idea or
have the feeling that something was wrong. In the bookstore, having the feeling that I am going home, I am torn
over buying the poetry books which are the most expensive ones: I wasn't sure I was staying. Am I? Yes I am.
No I can't. No I'm not. I want to put them back on the
shelves, but I buy them and I walk back to the dorm, in
the snow, in a daze. I have signed up for a poetry writing
class. It is what I can do, or all I can think of doing, and

I sit every night in front of a blank sheet of lined paper from after dinner to midnight unable to put down a line.

There is snow on the ground when I go to the bank to close my account and I feel like none of it is happening. Every grade in high school and before and the college scholarship and college search, all culminating in not being able to handle it.

I won't say good-bye. How can I explain why I am leaving? I'm still studying. The night lamp is dim and aimed at my bunk bed, but carved out in the shadow I can see everything the van will take away: my books, my tapes, my tape player, all the clothes in the closet and in the drawers, those bought in high school and those bought for college. This was supposed to be it. This is supposed to be the reason I sweated out nineties in high school, the extra credits, the extracurriculars. I'm leaving. I want to go away. I close my eyes and try to make it go away. Everything. Like I'm dead. Sleep nudges in for just a moment and then I come back to the room and look at the clock imagining that I might have slept three hours. It's 5:10. The van is that much closer and it won't stop, and it's like I'm still on the bus coming back to college after term break. I am the only one happy when the bus gets stuck in the snow. I want things to stop. I don't want to go back to school and I don't want to go back home. I just want to stay on the route we are on stuck in the snow until we have to resort to eating each other like Andes survivors. We play cards in the back of the bus but I can't concentrate on the game. I am thinking not only of time stopping because distance had stopped but I am hoping time will reverse: the bus goes backwards down the state route taking me back to New York City, to Brooklyn, to Canarsie, where I go back to high school, where I run for class honor society president, go back to junior high, go back to elementary school, kindergarten. The bus lunges out of the snow and we don't turn around.

The new term starts. It is colder. I am numb. I disguise myself from the friends I had made. I start taking the mental walks to the edge of the roof of the Arts Building, then I start to stop on the steps. It is the day that I stop on the steps for a long time that I call my mother. It is different from the other calls because I say hello and that's all I can say. She is crying on the other end, pleading with me to tell her what is going on, and then she hangs up. She calls back, having made the resolution that I am going home. I am in no condition to argue.

I shut myself in my room, afraid I will go out to the Arts Building before the van arrives. When I go to meals I walk quickly down the steps as if I am avoiding an oncoming car. I don't look at the Arts Building. I don't look at the view, but I don't pretend it isn't there. I think about it all the time. It is like having a revolver in my dresser drawer. Before I wasn't certain what I was upset about, but now I know. I am quitting, going home. Now at 5:20 in the morning on the day the van is coming, the revolver is still accessible to me. The roof of the Arts Building is open for use twenty-four hours a day. It doesn't need to be closed to be cleaned and it doesn't need to sleep. I can go out now . . .

An image slides into my head. It's me. Sitting on the bed a few days ago and opening my transcript, and finding very good grades and crying.

I mentally prepare myself. First a shirt. Then pants. Then a coat. Then the boots. I can go up now . . .

The phone rings. I don't believe it, so I just sit there and let it ring again. My roommate grunts and turns over in his bed. The phone rings again. I pick it up. It's my mother. She hasn't slept all night in anticipation of the move. She wants to know how I am. I say OK. She tells me she had trouble with the movers, that they didn't know how to get upstate, but that they should be there on time. Then she asks me how I am again. I say OK. She says that I shouldn't worry and that everything is going to be all right. She says she loves me very much. I say I haven't packed anything. She says I should if I can, but if I can't the movers will do it. It doesn't really matter how everything gets crated out. The most important thing is me. Everything else can be replaced.

I begin to cry. Then she begins to cry. Then she says again that she loves me very much and that everything will be all right when I get home. I'm going to go see a doctor and I'm going to get a job and I'll see that things will be all right. When everything has passed and cleared up, I can go back to school again. Then she says she'll see me when I get home, and we hang up.

I sit in bed trying to hold on to the idea that everything is going to be all right and I repeat it in my head. It sings. I look at the clock and it's almost 5:30.

## SUMMER 1982

I sit on the living room couch, looking out of the window in my house. Twilight. Canarsie. This is why I had to come home from school. It's starting here and happening in my head. An acid massage, all over my head, it's evil, relax, it's scouring you of evil. The devil is losing when you relax with it. There. He loses again to join the positive part of you.

I close my eyes and feel like a lantern, a beacon, if I open my eyes they would shine spotlights on the . . . I look into the television and see God. God is TV. God was always TV. God had been TV all the time.

There is no evil on television. If you knew the key you could read TV's secret message even in the commercials—THERE'S SOMETHING SPECIAL COMING THIS FALL! They are right and it's already here. They are talking about me and the new world. The world that starts right in this house, in my head, in Canarsie, at twilight.

I'll start building this new world, or even help it build itself, by vanquishing the wicked in me and vanquishing the wicked in this house.

Where would the wicked be? Evil smells evil, doesn't it? In the garbage, no (it's trickier than that), before it becomes garbage: in the refrigerator.

In thought I'm walking to the refrigerator three times before I realize that I'm not moving (I'll have to play beat-the-devil until morning) and then with two giant steps I'm there after casting the evil inertia aside.

What's in the fridge? I see it, in a jar, it stands out against all the other food. Deep red grape jelly in a jar, and I can prove the jelly is the devil in disguise in five metaphoric steps: Jelly—primordial slime—the beginning of consciousness—the tree of knowledge—the devil. I can prove it in color because red means danger and this jelly is a dark slimy blood clot of danger, and so I carefully dump it down the sink.

It sits in the drain unwilling to go down so I have to neutralize it with a gallon of white milk, but there's too much white and too much base and that creates its own problem, and so I modify the milk with a gallon of orange juice. Now the drain is a pool of liquid brimming at the sides the color and texture of fresh pus which proves the evil at the bottom is more potent than ever. I'm tempted to reach my hand in and shake the jelly loose but contact is a mistake and so I try to stir it out but the sides slosh over. Then I come up with an ingenious solution—wind. Didn't God put the finishing touches on his new world with a wind? I have the hair dryer. I go into the bathroom completely excited and get the hair dryer which I know given enough time will evaporate the pool in the sink without upsetting the jelly at the bottom.

It's while I'm stirring the sink with the hair dryer that the alarm in my mother's bedroom rings and she hears the hair dryer and comes in. She yells at me, asking what I am doing. How can I explain? So instead I tell her what I plan to do, which is to burn down the house if the hair dryer doesn't work. Now she's on the phone and I'm looking for the cooking matches in the kitchen drawer when I find a pair of batteries. Batteries. I can have a portable generator that radiates away evil. So I put the batteries in a big plastic cup and look in the fridge to see what would complement it and find honey. Honey-yellow—the color of the sun-solar power. I pour some honey into the cup, and my mother tells me that my father is coming to pick me up. She asks if I will burn down his house. I answer that I wouldn't if I didn't need to.

Now I am sitting on the porch with my batteries and honey waiting for my father. Why am I going to my father? Because my mother can't handle me. She is only equipped to handle me so far. My father is to take me the rest of the way. He'll lead me through this process of transformation. I'm ascending. Asendin, the drug the doctor gave me for depression, is for ascension—it's the drug for gods. It was really a placebo. The name is important—it's a hidden message—you're ascending, and it's true I am ascending. I'm going north from the southernmost tip of Brooklyn to my father's house somewhere else in Brooklyn. If necessary I'll take Brooklyn street by street until I reach Manhattan, Downtown, Midtown, Rockefeller Center, where I'll make my proclamation right by where I work in the mail room, where I began to ascend, walking around the streets on my lunch hour giving things away, buying things.

Now my father's pulling up. It's no coincidence he lives close by because everything is geared for this moment, now, so he could come when my mother called and take control. He's getting out of the car and he smiles at me. He knows about the new world and ascending. He knows. He looks at the cup and doesn't mention it as I take it along into the car. Now we go up the streets and we're taking Brooklyn street by street until we get to his house.

When we go inside, my grandmother greets us but the first thing I'm thinking is where I will put the cup of batteries and honey. It has to be a safe place and it has to be a place in the house where the energy of the house is right so its energy will spread. Not the windowsill although it would be the windowsill if there was afternoon. It isn't the living room, the bedroom . . . it's the dining room on the center of the table near the Sabbath candles. It looks right there and I put it down.

My grandmother asks me if I want something to eat and I know that she is leading me too and so I say yes, and she gives me some bread and butter and I eat although I'm not hungry because I know it's somehow important in the transformation.

My father asks me if I have to use the bathroom and I know that all their questions are leads, commands I'd best follow if I want to ascend. So I say yes and go. When I go in and they close the door I realize that this is another test. I look down into the toilet. That hole is the void that has to be filled. If it's the right thing it will be accepted and if it's the wrong thing it will be thrown back. I look around to see what's available to me and my eyes are attracted to the color of the aftershave. The color is green and it says Skin Bracer, and I think bracer is good and I pour it down the toilet. Now the toilet is very green. I flush it to see if the void will accept all of it and the toilet with a loud rumble accepts my sacrifice. I open the door and tell my father that I've passed, and he says good, and asks me if I want to lie down. I don't but I know this is another leading question and if lying down is important I will. I go into his bedroom and sit down on his bed and he helps me pull off my shirt and shoes like I was five again. I lie down and wonder where my transformation will lead and I begin to bray like a horse because I feel it's going that way. Now I can hear my grandmother crying in the living room and I think that's not an unusual reaction to saying good-bye to things.

My father holds me. He lays down on me as if to put out a fire on me, and with his arms around me in the dark of the bedroom he reminds me of a spider. We lay like that for a while and then a car horn beeps outside. My father helps me out, getting on my shirt and shoes, and as we're going outside my grandmother hands me a small Hebrew prayer book and kisses me on the cheek, she's still crying a little.

Downstairs my mother is waiting in the car and my father and mother don't speak to each other and I know this is part of the rules of the transformation. We pull away, ascending again, street by street going deeper into Brooklyn until we arrive at the hospital. It's light now and there are people on the street and I'm waving to them. My mother asks me why I am waving to them and I reply that they know me. They're people of faith, I can tell by looking at them. They know about my trans-formation.

In the hospital admissions room it is a story of those who are in the know and those who aren't. You could tell by looking at them, and by what they did. This is a crucial moment in the transformation and those in the know are focused on me or on protecting me. The guards are not protecting me. It's easy to tell by the way they hold themselves. They banter with each other, making jokes, and they walk around in place. There is a heavy woman in white by the desks, she stands com-pletely still with an emotionless face. She is the guard. She is protecting me.

I am reading the prayer book, my eyes half closed, and a Hasid comes by and twirls around two times, and I know he recognizes me. A woman who reminds me of my grandmother, a duplication, is tied up in a strait-jacket and screaming that she's been raped by the devil. I'm not afraid. I know my commission is to cure her, and so I yell out a cure for demonics based on the alpha-bet—A! A! A! B! B! B!, and she yells that I am a spy. The guards are confused by the display, but the woman in white is not. There is a big wasp flying near the ceiling and I know that it too is there protecting me. The guards try to shoo it away but it comes back, and I laugh. They interview me and I give them the name of the person I'm known as. When they ask me what languages I speak I say all of them, and the interviewer becomes annoyed. Now I'm taken upstairs, after being given my physical, and after that I wake up in a room.

I'm on a bed, and across from me is a man. He's smoking, he has a badly groomed beard and mustache, and is wearing a novelty shirt with pajama bottoms and paper slippers. I know immediately who he is. He tells me that I've been asleep for twenty-four hours, that they gave me Thorazine. Thor, I think, thunder pills. He tells me his name and then he begins to tell me about him-self. He was a stockbroker, had a black Coupe de Ville and a honey of an old lady. Now they are all gone. I can see he is a broken man. I broke him at the refrigerator and the toilet in my father's house. I ask him where his old lady is, and he says he doesn't know. I feel sorry for him, and I say I'll find her for him. I shouldn't have said that because now it's written in stone, and he laughs because he knows he's finally outsmarted me, pats me on the shoulder and says thank you. Then having won he complains about the showers and the food. I know the showers are cold but I don't really feel them, it's part of the transformation, and I can't complain about the food so long as they serve the right colors. He gives me back my prayer book, which he says I gave to him when I came in, but I know he stole it. He's just like the kind of pickpocket who'll pick your pocket and give back what he picked to show you he can pick it. My mother comes in and talks to him like she knows him too, thanking him for watching over me. She says it's time to go, and I ask how long I've been in this place, and she says a week. Now I know my mission will be side-tracked, that before I proclaim myself in Rockefeller Center I have to find the devil's mistress.

Not too long after I get home I get a phone call. It's from a friend I went to college with who is having a party in New Jersey and he asks me if I want to go. I know this is another leading question, that in fact I'm destined to go, so now I'm descending, descending into New Jersey, by train and bus, street by street, until I find myself at a phone outside a train station where my friend picks me up. The party has been going on for two days and every-body is working off their highs, lying around in the living room watching TV. I tell them I was hospitalized and that I'm now on Lithium, but that everything is all right, and they want to know what I was hospitalized for and I say fighting with the devil. This doesn't seem like insan-ity to them and they're not that impressed. My friend tells me that one of the women from college was there last night asking about me. That was it. The devil's mis-tress was looking for me as much as I was looking for her. She was on the other side of Jersey, but I don't know what that means in time and distance, I don't know it's a ninety-minute ride, and I don't know it's a thirty-dollar cab ride to her house, but it doesn't matter because I have no money anyway. What's most important is I have to get to her house, I have to get to her, at any cost, because it's an emergency, and she is the organ donor who can save my life if I can get to her. I might not ever get back to school to see her. The cab driver is lost. It's a backwoodsy place with no numbers on the houses, just names on the mailboxes, and it's dark and hard to see. When we finally find the mailbox with her last name on it I tell her the situation, borrowing the thirty from her which she had to get from her parents pissing them off at her, pissing her off at me, and pissing off the driver for giving him no tip. I'm calming her down in her big woodsy backyard. I'm promising to pay her back. I'm trying to explain my disappearance from school and what followed, all the time wanting not to alarm her but to confide in her, how it was all over and behind me now, gambling that she'd understand or at least take it as something to talk about after not seeing each other for six months: my horrible adventure and my enormous revelation.

I stopped. I sensed what was going on. She who knew me, who liked me, and didn't feel threatened by me and wasn't threatened by my story, knew I was different. I was talking rapidly. My eyes were unusually alive. I felt different to myself, but I liked it and I assured her I was all right.

I told her it's like having an LSD factory in my head. But it's all right now. It can be controlled. Really. The way I look at it, it happened and it's over. And if it recurs it's controllable, just a metaphor factory, it's a tap on creativity.

She doesn't seem to be alarmed but she looks worried. Now I realize I want her, and that this was all about the final temptation. We say good-bye when she

puts me on a train back to Manhattan. I tell her I'll see
her at school. I sit on the train thinking of song lyrics,
beaming over the fact that she kissed me, that it was all
coming true now and how I felt like I was one big YES to
everything. Wandering around the station at midnight
trying to get to the upper level, cursing myself because I
sat in the last car and now everyone had left the station,
every flight of stairs I take leads to a dead end. There are
stray cats all over the platform, I know they are only in
the form of cats, checking me out, and I finally reach the
surface and find a phone. I search my pockets. I forgot I
have no money. I have no money to get back home to
Brooklyn. I don't even have the money to buy a token. I
make a collect call to the mother of my old roommate,
she lives Uptown, and under the circumstances offers
to take me in.

I start on my way, walking down Lexington with a
cigarette and no match. There are stragglers on the
streets and the lights are so bright I should have sunglasses. They're beacons. Everything is a beacon. If a
man walks by in a coat it means something different
than if a man walks by in a hat and coat. Everything is
there to tell me where I am and where I have to go. Moving through the city is exploring, a voyage of discovery;
when something opens to you, you go with it. Don't get
distracted by the extraneous, the cats in the subway. I
am too distracted to realize I am signaling with an unlit
cigarette. A man comes up to me and asks me if I need a
light. We walk a while and I'm following him because
he's talking to me. I'm giving him my attention. He talks
to me up these steps. His apartment is full of African art
and there's a large book of poetry on a glass table. It's
obvious that's why I was brought here. The book rents
the apartment and the man works for it. I'm looking at

the book of poetry but he keeps telling me not to touch anything and he keeps talking and he's telling me all about himself but my mind is racing and I'm barely listening. He's in the bedroom and I go in and he is showing me porn on a video. Two black guys making it with a white blonde. She's very attractive. So far there's nothing I see that tells me to say no to any of this. All the while he's talking and my mind's going. He says he's a designer of children's clothes and he keeps talking and I keep interrupting him and I ask him what he does and he tells me again that he designs children's clothes. We're both sitting on opposite sides of the bed and he unzips his fly and begins to stroke himself, all the while talking, and asks that I do the same. The porno girl is working on me like VapoRub now. I'm not threatened by the designer of children's clothes but I won't let him touch me. I touch myself because I want to, because I'm really into the girl on the screen, and when I come I come to her and he doesn't seem displeased because when he ushers me out he tells me he liked it.

The streets glide under me all the way Uptown. It's late when I reach my roommate's house and I make up some story for his mother about being two hours late, some muggers, a chase, no money for the train, walking Uptown. My ex-roommate is home but already sleeping and I am put in his room but I can't fall asleep and spend the whole night going into the bathroom to jerk off, I can't stop jerking off, maybe I get an hour, maybe two hours, sleep.

Everything's an amusement park. Everything's a celebration. Walking up York Avenue heading for work in the morning talking to people, strangers, and getting them to talk back, especially women, minute meetings going down to Midtown on the East Side I realize I don't have the money to pay, but it's after I've eaten at the restaurant and what can I do, but this happens a lot and most managers just ask me for some ID as a marker with the idea that I'll come back the next day and pay my bill and get my ID back. The waitress gives me the check. I say I don't have the money to pay for it and I really am surprised that I don't have money, it never occurs to me that I have no money until I need it. She goes in the back and gets the manager and I offer this guy my watch (it is certainly worth more than the meal I just ate) and he starts screaming at me and throws me out of the restaurant telling me never to come back. I'm probably late for work, in fact I am, but there is a sign across the street that says "Spiritual Advisor. Palmistry." It jumps out at me, certainly they can see the something that I am heading for, it shows in my lifelines. It is time to be recognized as the Messiah. Even if I am late for work. I go up to the palm reader, it's above another store, now we shall find out if it's all true. The palm reader is a young girl about my age, not pretty, but I want her after being only a minute in her presence. She says some things that make no sense to me about silver and a bracelet, and I ask her if it's true psychics must be virgins. She says yes and that I can pay her now. I tell her that I don't have any money but can give her my watch. She excuses herself and goes back behind the curtain of beads and then returns. She says that I can keep my watch so long as I come back tomorrow and bring money. I agree.

Arriving at work, eluding my boss, I take the mail around that has been sitting in the mail room since nine. The offices take up the whole floor and I go office to office until I find myself in front of the office of my favorite secretary. I had once written her my version of a

Hallmark poem on a napkin—it is usual that my pockets are full of napkins and envelopes and other scraps of paper with poems on them—and I give it to her because she has such a beautiful smile.

I am feeling so high that I won't need to come on to anyone but now I imagine her in the office spread-eagled on her stomach with her skirt up over her back. I don't have to conjure up the image, it composes itself, it rolls back like a mechanized sardine can.

I say I had a great weekend. That is a lie, the week ran into the weekend and the weekend ran into the week. There is no more calendar, it is just a matter of time before everyone else catches on. I am asked to help someone out at the copy machine, a woman, I don't even know her name, and soon we are laughing and joking around and she never has had so much fun at the copy machine. We even go out to lunch together. I had just got to work and it's time for lunch—time sure has abandoned us all. She takes me shopping for herself, and when we return I go into the mail room and find a delivery envelope in the basket, so I decide to take it out for a delivery run and end up in the movies. It is a film called *This Is Not a Love Story,* about exploitation in pornography, and it shows the photography tricks, including how a woman's vagina is just about turned inside out for a snatch photo and how uncomfortable it is, even painful, and it seems sad and I cry and dry my face with some poems. There are a lot of things that can move me to tears. It is always warm and cathartic. When I return to the office, I realize that I'm still holding the envelope I was supposed to deliver, and so I put it back in the outgoing mail basket. It is almost time to go and I think I'll write some poetry in the office, when the woman I went to lunch with comes into the mail room.

She says not to talk like that to her again, and she leaves. I don't remember saying anything to her but it doesn't matter because before I know it I am on the train heading home, going into the bedroom and, stripping down to my underwear, laying out on the bed every *Playboy* I have, along with my high school yearbook, and if that doesn't do it nothing will, and then my mom opens the bedroom door interrupting me.

She says she wants me to go back to the hospital. I agree but say that I have to see the Gypsy. She makes me promise to stay in the house. I say I will stay in the bedroom and contact the Gypsy by levitation. But I decide instead to purify my bedroom book collection. Bad books on my brother's bed and good books on mine. *Dracula*, definitely an evil book. *Slaughterhouse-Five*, death, an evil book. *Tropic of Cancer*, disease, an evil book. *Lord of the Flies*, Beelzebub, definitely evil. *Compulsion*, evil. *Zen and the Art of Motorcycle Maintenance*, enlightenment, good. *For Whom the Bell Tolls*, judgment day, good. *The Last Tycoon*, the end of money, good. *Steppenwolf*—when the book is in doubt, think about the title, it sounds evil and is an evil book. The dictionary—will eventually be extraneous when everybody is telepathic and there is no use for writing, so it is a book of this age which is an evil age, therefore it is evil. The dictionary hits the bedroom wall with a slam that brings my mother back in. She asks what I'm doing. I say that I am cleaning. She says that she thought I was going to levitate.

I look at her, not hateful of her ignorance, just tired of it. I tell her the room must be pure before the levitation. Rather than continue the discussion, my mother closes the door. Later I will go to the hospital and this makes sense to me. Where would the Messiah be if not curing the ill? The question of what to wear is more important. I go into my closet looking for something white and come up with my old karate suit. Perfect. Now I feel I need a sign, a sign upon my forehead. I take some red acrylic paint from the tube and dab it on my forehead as a third eye. Now it is time to go to the hospital.

My mother takes me in her car and I wave to my minions like before and when we get to the hospital grounds I eat leaves from a tree because it is not enough just to see how beautiful it is. We go inside and sit in a waiting area.

There is a man sitting beside me with red hair; he is a little heavy and he sticks out his hand and introduces himself to me. I introduced myself as Christ, and he says he is glad he found me because he is the sinningest man in the world. He goes on to describe his list of crimes from stealing chalk from the chalkboard to bank robbery. I say that I can help him.

Then they take me into a room and ask me questions. They ask me how I am feeling, and I think to tell them that I have discovered that my soul is eternal but it comes out that if you set me on fire I will not die. They take me inside the electronic doors and my mother leaves.

In my room there are two beds and I know one is for the devil and one is for me. There is a small bathroom with a toilet and I see the void in it and so I fill it with what's available—paper towels. The void rejects it and water comes spilling over the rim into the room and into the hall. A nurse comes over and says to call maintenance and she asks me why I did that and I say that I have to give sacrifice. She tells another nurse to get that dot off my head and that while she is at it she should give me a bath.

Now I know it is time and I feel peaceful and alive. I ask the nurse if I am chosen to get a bath and she says that I am getting a bath. This is my baptism. I ask the nurse if his name is John and he says his name is Jack and I think of the variations that play through the second coming.

Jack sits on the rim of the bath while I wash myself and he tells me about his family and his wanting to become a nurse and that I should take good care of myself while I am in the hospital. I say I will and I say that I appreciate his life. When the bath is over the sucking noise of the water going down the drain reminds me of the void and the devil and I get out fast. I put on new clothes from my bag and go into the dayroom.

The first person I meet is a girl, probably a little younger than me, who says her name is Gabrielle. I ask if she is the archangel and she says it is the same name. I talk with Gabrielle for a while and then I see the sinningest man sitting on the couch and I go over to him. He asks me about the archangel and says that he'd like to wear her vagina for a hat, but he sees her with someone else.

I know it is time that I look for the devil in whatever new form he takes. Look for the position of power. Sure enough there is a meeting of the patients and the leader has to be the devil. He is tall and thin, with dark hair, and is a chain smoker going under the name of Sammy, and it is the devil who is courting the archangel Gabrielle. After the meeting I watch the devil sitting and smoking with the archangel. He is analyzing her problems and giving her free will as a tool to get his way. He says that she can leave her house and come live with him if she hates her father, and the archangel seems to be swayed. Then the devil leaves to get more cigarettes and the sinningest man moves in. He introduces himself to the archangel and tells her of his exploits and he is funny and she laughs and laughs.

When he leaves the archangel comes over to me and says that both the devil and the sinningest man asked her to go into the music room alone and she asks me what she should do. I say to go with the sinningest man because that is the lesser of two evils. Someone, a male voice, calls my name and I look around, and my world shatters and is re-created. This is the devil. Sam has to be only a demon. This man has a goatee and heavy eyebrows and a buttoned-down shirt and dress slacks and he says his name is Doctor Natis. It is close enough to be Satan spelled backwards, and is certainly the high position of power. We go into his office and he asks me how I am feeling and I say I feel as good as Christ and ask when I will be discharged. He says I will be eventually. I don't believe him. He promises. I say I won't take his verbal promise, I want it in writing. So he gives it to me. I have beaten the devil at every step and now I know I have conquered him.

Then I look at Doctor Natis and somehow he doesn't seem like the devil to me anymore. He said we're here to take care of you at the hospital, and that thought infuses itself in my head. The trials are over. I want to reach out to him and thank him for taking care of me. It is over, and when I walk out of the hospital on my discharge day it will be totally over. I smile and he smiles back at me. Everything is going to be fine.

## WINTER 1983

The radio is playing Joe Jackson's "Steppin' Out." The couple in the song are escaping the doldrums and gloom again by stepping out into the night. The station that the radio is tuned to plays the top ten songs, and every day it's the same songs. I didn't tune the radio to that station. A Federal Express man came in one day and turned it on after saying I needed to liven up the place. The radio is by the door on top of a locker and it's too far away. Too far away from where I'm sitting to get up and go over and stop it. And too much effort to re-tune it.

I close my eyes and balance myself tilting back in the bad wooden chair screening out everything, thinking of nothing, sitting with my eyes shut the way people do on the subway. The chair tips too far and I have to pull it back into balance. This time, in the morning, in the basement, is the easiest time of the day because I don't have to face anyone. Almost no one comes in to get the mail and if I balance adroitly on the chair and squeeze my eyes shut I can almost go away. I keep the door to the mail room shut to discourage them, to make them think the mail room is closed and to drown out the boiler room which is down the hall. With the door closed the air is stagnant and the only light comes from one bulb on the ceiling. I sit in the circle of dingy yellow light and everywhere else in the room it is dark. I feel secure. I don't have to move.

I have a big wooden desk, and behind me there is a block of mail shelves and unless the postal worker comes to deliver the mail I'm alone except for the mouse that is trapped in the glue tray underneath the mail shelves and against the wall. My feelings for the mouse are small and shriveled. I can feel some sympathy but it is far away, deep down, trying to climb up the rungs of a ladder and falling, falling. The mouse writhes and twitches, kicks a few times and as I check on it I know it is becoming more stuck and slowly starving to death.

The aim is to get to the threshold of sleep, a gluey sleep, a cheese melt, a nod and then resurface as close to noon as possible. I come back up to check my wrist-watch and find it's only ten to ten, so I go back in before I can think I'm here and why I'm here and where I should be and why I'm not there, at school. I know I have to get back, but I'm afraid I won't, I can't, not the way I am now. I have to be careful not to let these thoughts get too close. They hurt. I have to be careful. The chair is important. If it tilts too far on its back legs I can fall over and easily bust open my head.

I try again. Closing my eyes. Tilting back. A picture jumps in. It's the Arts Building covered with snow and I remember. I shut it off squeezing my eyelids. I block as hard as I can to take the image away.

Nothing matters. Nothing. Nothing. Nothing.

The image fades because it doesn't matter, because nothing matters, not school, not my job, not my mother, brother or father, not me. This feels safe and good. It stops the pressure for a moment, a pressure that says that everything matters so strongly that I should do

something about it but I can't. I squirm under the pressure. It says: DO SOMETHING! DO SOMETHING NOW!
again and again and I feel myself screaming without
making a sound. I fall back on the cadence:
NOTHING MATTERS. NOTHING. NOTHING.

I believe it and it's restful. I tilt back in the chair and
erase my mind. It's a blank screen now and I stare into
it hypnotized. When I come up and look at my watch
it's 11:30. Milk this half hour. The door opens. It's the
mailman. He's about my age. In uniform. My eyes snap
open. He says good morning. I say good morning back.
I don't try to smile because it takes too much. I can
summon it but all I get is a twitch at the corners of my
mouth. The smile climbs the ladder, and fails, falling, I
don't believe it.

He works around me, filling the mail slots. If he's
thinking, his thoughts are not distracting him to slow
him down the way mine are. He seems to be moving
in fast motion. When he's done he moves toward the
door. In passing, looking at me, he asks if I had a hard
night. I must look bad. I lie that I'm not getting enough
sleep.

The thoughts spring up, about why I look so bad, why
I can't move like everyone around me. I tilt too far back
and lose balance and, compensating, throw myself forward, my fists balled against the desk. Why did you
have to leave college? Look where you are now. Why
can't you smile? Why did you leave? Look at yourself.
Your life is going by, second after second. I kick back
in the chair, squeezing my eyes shut tightly as if my
thoughts are projected on the wall in front of me and I
can't bear to see them. I regain balance in the chair. I
repeat the cadence that takes everything away and I'm
away.

Everything is erased. No thoughts. No time. Then it's broken, when I come up it's 11:35, and then 11:41, and now it's too close to try for more. The mail room key, a rusty gold thing, is on the table and I put on my corduroy coat that was draped over the chair. I take my book. I put the key in my coat pocket and leave without turning off the radio.

The basement corridor is dark like the mail room and I can hear the boiler churning as I pass the boiler room, and then I go past a half-closed door with a rusty slop sink. All the time I know where I'm headed and I can feel the resistance from my legs because I'm going to the stairs and up to the offices where there are people. There are ten steps up to the main floor and I stop at the halfway point, at the fifth step. Now I have to convince myself to keep going. Telling myself that standing on the fifth step between the basement and the main floor is an impossible and ridiculous protest is not enough. I have to remind myself what this is all about: you go from one station alert and fighting the thoughts, to the next station asleep—from bed to train to mail room. They'll find you. They'll find you on the steps standing here. What will you say? How can you run now? Where is your next place?

I will drop off the key at the office, making my way through the faces, hoping no one says anything to me that requires a response, and then I will go to lunch. My legs are bribed successfully and after waiting for and hearing the go command in my head, my legs take me up the final five steps.

The light is different on the main floor. It is all fluorescence and daylight. In front of the office is one of the security guards. He's wearing a red uniform and has a toothpick in his mouth. I walk stiffly, my hands close to

my sides and slightly raised like a robot. I move slowly.
He greets me, playing with me in a mocking way, he
calls me Speedy and I say hello deferentially, head
bowed.

In the office behind the desk is a heavy woman with
long fingernails that make it necessary for her to use
a pencil to dial the phone. She runs the office but the
hierarchy here confuses me. It's obvious that it's one of
the group of men that go in and out of the office and
that the men in suits are on the top with the men in
uniforms on the bottom below the secretaries. The
woman with the long fingernails smiles and asks me
how it is going in the mail room. I want to say difficult
but I can't because I couldn't explain why but I really
want to say it. I say fine.

I hand in my key and go to lunch. With no one to talk
to and nothing to do provided you don't read, I sense the
employees realize what an intolerable job the basement
mail room is for someone with normal needs. No one
else wants to do it. It's the easiest job for me.

Lunch is the only time of day that doesn't hurt. I
should carry a bag lunch to save money but it's my one
pleasure of the day to go to a restaurant. It's a pleasure
because it's free of pain. I put food and eating between
me and my thoughts. There is a Chinese restaurant and
a vegetarian one a block away from the offices, and I
alternate between them.

Making that block is hard, but I drive myself, passing the raised concrete and the parking lot, I'm going
out to lunch and out of myself again. Today I'm in the
vegetarian place. I'm sitting at the table looking at the
waitress who is by the door. She is short, with a short
haircut and big earrings. Her dress is a floral pattern.
She seems the type of person I might meet at school

when I get back there. She comes over to the table and I think she is going to take my order, but instead she asks me if I am cold. Should I be cold? Why is she asking this? I want to be normal. I want to fit in. I don't want to make waves or draw attention to myself. I say no. She says that she asked because I am shaking. I say that I hadn't noticed and that I'm sorry. She says that I don't have to be sorry, and I realize that I've overextended myself in the apology. Then I say that I'm all right to reassure her. She offers to move me to another table further away from the draft of the door. I say that I'm all right.

Thankfully the waitress leaves. Now that my Haldol shake has been noticed I'm nervous and the shake becomes even more exaggerated. I spill some water. The waitress returns. She says that it would be no inconvenience for me to move. The restaurant is empty except for me. I say that I'm OK. The waitress takes my order and leaves, then returns with the manager. The manager insists that he move me to the back of the restaurant away from the door to where I'll be more comfortable.

I agree. When I get to the back table my shake continues, my hands shake holding the soyburger, my fork clinking the plate while I manipulate the bed of romaine lettuce and carrot shreds. The waitress returns. She asks me if I'm all right. I say yes, trying to cover. She asks me if I'm sure. I say yes. She says that she's asking because I'm still shaking. I say everything's fine, and I hurry up and finish, fleeing, crossing over the street to the small park outside the office building.

I'm alone with the bushes, sitting on the concrete square and it's cold but I hardly feel it. I'm holding my book. I look at my watch. Ten to one. My hands tremble.

A sparrow bounces along the concrete and I watch it, feeling alone. I try to stop my hands from trembling by putting them under my thighs. No one will come to the park. It is too cold. I should be back in school. I've failed.

I zero out staring at the sparrow and then I look at my watch. Seven to one. I'm sitting alone in the cold in the park. The sparrow flies away and now I am completely alone in the concrete park. My hands are shaking and I put them back under my thighs. Cars go by on First Avenue and some people are walking by and I feel out of touch with everything. Not distanced. Lost. The minute hangs and then it's one o'clock.

I slowly go to another office on the ground floor. There's a coffeepot there and I have three cups of coffee and still I feel listless. My job is to sit behind a desk and wait for phone calls from people who are interested in receiving a prospectus. I can do this. I can write down information on blue cards and take messages for the sellers who work out of the office.

Today there is someone in the waiting area. He's middle-aged and wearing a suit. He says hello to me. That response is simple. Say hello back—Hello. He says it's a nice day. Agree—I say it's a nice day. He asks me if I was on the phones once in another building. I was better then. I was on the switchboard. I was a perfect conversationalist. They loved me. I tell the man in the waiting area that I wasn't that man. He disagrees. Then I am saved by one of the sellers who takes the man into his office. How could I explain that I may look like the person at the switchboard but I'm not the same person? I can't talk like that person did.

There is no sleeping here but I stare into space and put the book in front of me in case anyone passes by. I have another cup of coffee. I stare. I look at my watch.

There are no phone calls. Soon the man will come out of the office and he will probably say something to me, like good-bye, say good-bye. I lock my eyes on the wall, hypnotizing myself. There is something, a thought, I can't say it, I can't think it and I don't know it as it is passing. It's always there but I work so hard all day to keep it away, on the periphery, and I keep moving, keeping it away.

When the man leaves he only says good-bye and it is not necessary to make a response. The sellers are in their offices and when they come out they will dismiss me. The phone may ring and it may not. There is a lot of staring to do. Even with my wristwatch to anchor me, I lose the sense of time, and I have to keep looking at it. When one seller comes out of her cubicle to dismiss me for the day I don't know if it's been a long time or a short time. She is the seller I like, heavy-set, frosted perm, almost motherly, she tells me to have a good night and I just look at her. She asks me if something is wrong, and I want to tell her but I can't. I can't explain it and I can't let on. I say no and put on my corduroy coat and leave with my book.

It's three blocks to the subway and they seem very long. I measure myself by the furniture store—the furniture store is halfway. All between are brownstones, then there's the furniture store, then brownstones, and then Lexington Avenue and the subway. Brownstones. Furniture store. Brownstones. Subway. I move against the resistance, making it to the subway because I have to do it. At the subway I wait for the train, and I sit on the bench not wanting to get on. The people all around me look impatient, staring down the tracks. They want to get home or at least they don't want to wait. It makes sense to them. I break down. I don't want to get up. I don't want to move. I want to stop. I want this to stop here on this bench in the subway station. As the light of the train comes down the track, the thought that finally gets me up is not one of routine, or the thought of something pleasurable at the other end of the work week. The thought is that if I sit on this bench not getting up no one will come and get me. The train will pass and then no one will come and rescue me. No one will hear my protest. I get on the train, which is rush hour packed.

I have to switch trains at Union Square and then I walk some more, and it's rough. Then there's the L. It's packed. Third Avenue. First Avenue. The tunnel. In the tunnel I try to zero out as the fluorescent lights go out in the train but it would be easier sitting down and I won't get a seat until the middle of Brooklyn. The lights go on again. I look around. There are faces. I don't have to respond to them. They ask nothing of me, but I can feel even in their subway masks that they are somewhat happy to be going home. I have to sit down, but I can't sit down. I'm not elderly or handicapped and I have no excuse. I have no priority. I close my eyes and feel my own weight. I'm holding it up, holding tightly to the pole that is covered with hands.

The train stops. This is not the stop where everyone gets off, but it's beginning to empty. A seat opens and although I've positioned myself to get it, I'm too slow to move and I lose it. I feel the pressure of my own weight coming down over my head and then my shoulders and driving into the floor of the subway car through my shoes. Take it. Take it. Hold on. Then another seat opens like a miracle right in front of me and I let myself drop into it.

I zero out and for a while it's just passing shadows, with my eyes closed, the sound of the train, the stops, and the sounds of people getting off. When the train stops for good, it's Rockaway Parkway. Last stop. The car empties of its remaining passengers and I move along. Now it's very cold and I feel it. It's dark. I hunch my shoulders, chin to coat collar like a turtle and move along telling myself it's not too far now. Outside of the station my mother will be waiting for me in the car because I can't walk the five blocks it takes to get home. I get out of the station and pick out the old blue Buick and go to it. The windows are fogged up and the car is running so it doesn't stall. I get in at the passenger side and close the door. My mother has a face that says it's been a tough week and she says that she's glad it is Friday. We ride silently and pull up at the house. After making it up the stairs I go directly to bed without taking my shoes off. I stare at the ceiling. I can hear my mother in the kitchen, the sound of running water in the sink, but it's not diverting enough to drown out the thoughts. Do something. Do something. I have to make it go away, and I force myself to sleep.

When I come up my brother is in his bedroom in the next room. We share a wall and I hear him getting ready to go out for Friday, or is it Saturday night? My room is very dark. My room is always dark with the shades drawn but it is especially dark in the evening. He's talking on his phone, making plans with his friends and I think about going out. A few images of going out surface and I push them down. I could never go out, to move around, to talk to people. Being sad about it climbs up in me a few rungs and then it falls. I just have to survive. I push it all down and close my eyes again. When I wake up it is pitch black. There's no light coming through the bottom of the bedroom door from the kitchen. No sounds. My mouth is dry, I let it tug-of-war with my need to stay put, but it is so dry it forces me up out of bed and into the kitchen for a drink from the refrigerator.

Now the kitchen is dark and my brother's door is closed. I look up at the clock. It's four o'clock in the morning. He could still be out or he could be sleeping after going out. I don't know if it's Saturday morning or Sunday morning, or even Monday morning. There's food in the refrigerator, cold chicken, but I'm only thirsty.

I have my drink and go back to bed but I can't get back to sleep. The pillow is damp on both sides. It gets that way when I sleep on it too much. I must have rotated it, and every time I try to get myself to sleep I feel pins and needles in my hands. I lie in bed and the thoughts edge their way in. Do something. Do something. They chase me back to the kitchen where I take a piece of cold chicken even though I have no appetite. I'll block the thoughts with food like I do at lunch. I go into the dining room and sit down at the dining room table without turning on the light. I eat the chicken even though I don't want it, because if I concentrate on the chewing the thoughts take a backseat.

But when I'm done and I've eaten and was not hungry the thoughts come back. I can't go to sleep. I can't concentrate on television, a book or music, there's no diversion possible. I count the hours until Monday morning. If it's Monday it is four hours until I have to wake for work, if it's Sunday, oh God let it please not be Sunday. I move to another chair in the dining room just to do something. Nothing's different here. I sit for a while blocking and then I move into the living room. Blocking. Blocking. I have to piss, and that's something to do like eating and drinking and I go into the bathroom and piss while looking at the sink, and there is my razor.

It all comes up like vomit in my head. This is intolerable and if this is intolerable then why go on with it? I finish pissing and feel the gates shut tight in my head. I climb into bed and snuggle with the blanket pretending that I can't move to protect myself from going back into the bathroom. I feel the pins in my hands but I push through them fighting my way back to sleep. Sleep. Sleep. Sleep. I beg my way back. When I wake it's lighter outside and so I go into the bathroom to get ready for work not looking at the razor. A shower is too difficult and so I put some water and soap under my arms, put on a clean shirt, and go back to bed thinking I don't want to go to work. I don't want to go to work, but let it be Monday.

## WINTER 1984

Someone once told me that someday I would know the meaning of my life. And now I do!

It didn't happen once but twice. The first time was interrupted and now it is here to complete itself. I found the key to my life by unlocking the key to everything. It comes to me in flashes of a code in numbers, letters, and colors. Light bulbs powered by sound, light bulbs to be outstared by the power of my mind and eye, the imprint of the blue tungsten coil that I watch for a whole night.

I am something truly special with a purpose to fulfill, perhaps a prophet, perhaps the Messiah. Running from catalyst to catalyst and sleeping no more than half an hour a day, and eating no more than half a meal.

I can outstare light bulbs.

I can.

I've been up three days practicing. I don't sleep. This is better than sleep. I look a long time at the bulb, staring it down, and it makes itself visible to me. First it shows a bright orange halo like a corona of the sun (it's defending itself), but I persist, and then it shows its hot electric blue coil and I have to stare at that until it snaps. I haven't blown one out yet, but it takes a long time, and I can see it begin to blacken already.

It's January and it is snowing outside. I'm wearing a pair of yellow goggles and everything's bright and electric, it almost seems like the particles in the air are racing all around me, and the atoms are spinning in their orbits and I could put my finger between them if I want to.

Feeling like God, being God, means being on all the time, slowing down is a problem, sitting in a bar with strangers who have no idea of the change that's overtaken me, I'm drinking liquor, beer, Guinness stout, to slow me down, because it's hard to manage this head.

I'm working on an antigravity suit. The preliminary sketches are already done. When it's finished I will fly it over to Washington, D.C., and declare world peace on the White House lawn.

I'm in the living room lying on the carpet with the earphones on and the volume at ten and still it's too low. I'm holding my harmonica, my ram's horn. My mother and brother are sleeping and have no idea of the mission I must undertake. They're in their bedrooms and the rooms make them ignorant. Rooms have that effect. I go from room to room feeling the difference in their boundaries. I am restless.

In the bathroom I turn on the light and stare into the mirror experimenting with my stare. With one eye closed staring into that eye for less than a minute, the world goes dark. A black cloud forms around the eye that is being stared into and the blackness is primal. I must record these experiments and at the same time I know I must not be distracted from my mission. I smile realizing that one will lead into the other and I go into the bedroom looking for paper.

There is a stack of papers, school papers, telephone numbers, and under the stack I find my college brochure and a photograph inside it gives me the answer. It is the arch. The Washington Square Park arch will be my launching pad, and I'm amazed how when if you need to know an answer you find it. Still, the arch is a train ride away and so I get dressed like anybody going to work, and walk to the train beaming, happy to do my job.

It's morning rush hour and cold and everyone's breath is filling the car. I look around me to see if there's somebody on the line I know and I scan the car for body parts. There's an arm that might be attached to a face I might know but the face doesn't match, and there's a leg that's attached to a head I might know but the face doesn't match. Then I see buttocks in jeans and I know I recognize them and so I tap the person on the shoulder and it is Jill. She says hello and remembers me from high school. We talk and I don't divulge my true identity or my mission and when she has to get off the train she gives me her address and says good-bye.

How does Jill fit in? I don't know, I'll have to wait and see.

The train pulls in at Union Square and I get off and change trains for 8th Street. When I get on campus I don't go straight to the park because you never approach things directly, you have to romance yourself to them with sidesteps.

I go up to the magazine office where I work to see if anyone's there and sure enough one of the editors is behind the desk. We start talking and I know him pretty well and can trust him so I tell him about one of my missions. I tell him about the light bulb powered by ambient sound and he says that if I really believe in it I should check it out with the physics department. When I go he asks me if I am really going there because he was just kidding, and I tell him I don't turn down leads.

Now, I'm in the physics building and I know the offices but I don't know the professors so I choose from their names on their doors, picking words that are comprised of more benign letters than malevolent ones. I find my door and knock on it, and a voice calls me in. I go in and introduce myself as a student and say that I have an idea for an invention of an ambient-sound-powered light bulb and he says that it's an unmanageable idea. He says that anyone who told me that I could make an ambient-sound-powered light bulb was crazy, and then he goes on for half an hour about the physical problems of such an endeavor and lectures on physics and suggests that I take his class.

I thank him and leave heading for the park when I run into another friend from the school magazine who suggests that we go to a bar, so because I never turn down an offer like that we do. I'm drinking Guinness stout and I can feel it slowing my God head. I want to ask him how to get to the top of the arch because I realize that this is why I met him, but I want to lead up to it and so I spend two hours leading up to it and then come out with it just as we're leaving. He asks me if I want to jump off the arch, and my mind reels—he's a prophet and a mind reader as well and so I say yes, and he laughs and says good-bye.

Now, here I am so close but so far from taking off to the White House, and I'm certain the world is waiting for my arrival, and there is a piece of the puzzle sticking out—Jill. Why did I meet her today? And soon the question becomes so strong within me that I'm back on the train to Brooklyn holding that piece of paper with her address on it.

The liquor is beginning to wear off and I know it's because I'm going back to Brooklyn. The atoms spin and

my head races as I find the house that Jill lives in and
ring the bell. When she sees me she is a little taken
aback but glad and I think this is the proper greeting for
me.

We go into her apartment and are talking in the bedroom and there are pictures of Jesus all over the room,
and I know why I am here. Jill tells me that after high
school she broke up with her boyfriend who was a
drunk and abused her, the devil himself, and Jesus
saved her life.

I sit in Jill's bedroom discussing Jesus. We're looking
at a picture of the Last Supper and I know that Jesus is
not in the center of the picture, he is not at the center of
the table, he is the man to the right of the man at the
center of the table and I want Jill, but Jill doesn't believe in premarital sex since she found Christ. She says
she came close once but a black hole came up and almost swallowed her. She didn't actually see that black
hole but it was a stifling feeling, the feeling of sin.

And I wonder what Jill would say if I asked her what
she would do if Christ asked to fuck her, but I don't
have to ask because I know if Christ asked to fuck her
then he wouldn't be Christ, then he would surely be the
devil in disguise, and so even though I am Him there is
no way to get at this, so it must be me who feels wrong
or I'm really not Christ, but I am Christ and so I wonder
if there is a compromise: and I imagine us both, me and
Jill at opposite ends of the bedroom, in her closed bedroom, naked, sitting in the lotus position having sex
without touching.

She tells me she is planning to go to a church meeting
in downtown Brooklyn and I want to go. I will be recognized for certain. When the meeting begins the preacher
talks about me and there's music and prayer but the

part that irritates me is when the people get up and start to speak in tongues. It makes me uncomfortable and I walk out on what I consider an inappropriate worship.

I reach into my pocket and find a poem I must have written last night and it strikes me that this is as good a way as any to spread my word, and I wrote and found the poem for a reason.

Now I'm on the train heading back to campus to get my poem published, but it's night, and so I realize what I'm supposed to do is ride the train all night until morning.

The cars are almost empty but in one car I find a man. His eyes are glassy and crossed and he sits hunched over and his tongue is a little out of his mouth. I go to him and extend my harmonica, which I pull from my pocket, curing him in a way that I know will take time to happen. There are other passengers on the train and they watch the healing and then look away. They will spread the word. They are apostles.

Morning. School. I go back to the building where my magazine office is and right next door (how could I have missed it?) is the poetry office. I knock on the door. No one's there. I've come to a dead stop. I think I must have missed something and it holds itself out to me—I already have my word spread. Last semester I handed in my cinema studies paper with a broken French message written on the cover—*Je sais qui*. Now the paper must be ready to be picked up and the message has gone through. I go to the cinema studies office and there are students milling about in the lounge and the head of the department who has gotten my message is in his office on the phone. He seems to be talking about a documentary on the Holocaust and I want to go in and tell him that there was a reason I wasn't there but I don't want to interrupt him.

My head is racing. The thoughts are pounding through like elephants—why did you abandon the people of the Holocaust? why do you abandon anyone? I feel myself beginning to cry and I decide to go downstairs and get a drink and then come back up again. In the bar after ordering my drink I realize that I have no money left. DAMN THIS MATERIAL PLANE! DAMN IT! The guy next to me sees me going through my pockets pulling out shreds of paper and my harmonica. I say right out to him that I can't pay for this beer. He says that it's OK and gives me the money for the one beer. I don't know how to thank him. I offer my harmonica but he says to keep it.

The thoughts have slowed down a little and I remember Jill. I walked out on her. I have to apologize, so I'm back on the train, jumping the turnstile, heading for Brooklyn, and the alcohol begins to wear off at First Avenue again, and I get to Jill's house and nobody's home.

Where could she be? In church. I go back on the train jumping the turnstile, back to the church, which is closed. What do I do now? I have to go to Jill's place and sit vigil by her door. Back on the train. I have to vindicate myself for all the atrocities of mankind and begin by apologizing to Jill. Jill's apartment. I ring the bell and there's a light on in the hallway.

Jill's home! She greets me at the door and lets me in. We go into the bedroom and two friends are sitting there, a woman with a short haircut and a man with a red sweater. She introduces me. They say hello and quickly initiate me into their discussion about Christ. The man is leading and I ask him why the Holocaust happened and he looks at me and says to read Job, and

I counter with would you tell Christ to read Job and he says that it's possible Christ did read Job. Then we talk about Judas. He says that Judas could not be held responsible for his actions because he was Judas and it was his nature to betray. I say that if Christ came back, his wish would be to forgive the second coming of Judas. The circle laughs but I know I have just written my next mission. The discussion goes on until about midnight when the circle breaks up and I'm left alone with Jill, who ushers me out saying she'd love to talk some more but she has work in the morning.

I'm out in the street. It's snowing. Cold. Go home. It's not far. Go work on your flying suit and your ambient sound light bulb, go work on the way to cure all diseases and make water and food out of dirt, go home.

I reach into my jacket pocket for my yellow glasses and I find a ten dollar bill folded into a tight square. This is for my search for Judas and this is for shelter and the ten dollars tells me I have to go somewhere where it will take ten dollars to get there. Ronald. Ronald lives on Staten Island and to get to his house I'll have to take a train and the ferry and a cab that will cost close to ten dollars. He'll put me up for the night and he'll help me find Judas.

I'm back on the train again looking at every passenger for signs that one might be Judas. I know he might be bashful, he might be hiding, he might try to run from me and this makes the search all the harder. He might not be a he at all. He might be a woman. He might be a child. He might be old. He might be very young. All I know is that he will somehow betray me again.

The train has no Judas. Maybe there's a Judas on the Staten Island ferry. I go from seat to seat, from area to area, looking. I know he will recognize me and probably run, so I look for sudden movements in the passengers when I go by. I look for people who are trying not to be seen. There are possible suspects but no one seems to be exact so I go to the rail and look over the water thinking this will be hard. There are millions of people just in this city and I'm on a two-thousand-year-old mission without a clue. The only thing I can do is have faith that I'm moving in the right direction, that, being Christ, Judas will be attracted to me because I must find him.

The ferry pulls into dock and I get off and find a cab taking me to Ronald's. When I get there he's surprised to see me but happy and he asks me what I'm doing in Staten Island. I come right out with it, I tell him that I'm on a search to find the second coming of Judas. Ronald asks me if I mean to kill anyone. I laugh and say that I mean to forgive Judas when I find him.

We go in the house and Ronald, who rents the downstairs basement, says I can stay the night and then he goes off to use the bathroom. I hear him talking to himself through the wall but I can't hear what he is saying and then when he comes back I ask him what he was saying to himself while he was in the bathroom, and he says he always talks to himself while he is in the bathroom and that he talks about nothing in particular. Then he asks me to tell him about where I've been and what I've seen and who I am now. I tell him everything and we talk a long while until there is a knock at the door. He goes to answer it and it's my mother and brother with terribly serious looks on their faces.

I look at Ronald and it all crashes down on me. I feel grace and joy and my eyes become wet as I see poor Ronald hanging from that noose two thousand years ago. I hug him and kiss his cheek and I forgive him and then I say good-bye and go with my mother and brother.

Going over the Verrazano Bridge my mother is quiet but my brother is cursing me. He says he's going to put me in my room and tie me up with rope until the morning comes because I'm not running around anymore, and he can't afford to accompany my mother on another trip to who knows where again. My mother says I'm going to the hospital in the morning. I'm beaming. I forgave Judas.

## SUMMER 1984

The space for movement in the deli is no bigger than an elevator. By the entrance there is a large refrigerator where the beverages are kept, a mirrored wall that was mirrored in an effort to make the space look bigger, and a column in the center of the floor which is also mirrored. Opposite is the counter with the countermen behind it, and squeezed into the back are the women who work the phones. I'm in line with the rest of the runners waiting for the lunch deliveries. The line starts by the phones, curves around the column, and extends out the door. I sit on a fire hydrant outside the deli saving my legs as best I can. When I deliver I don't run, I don't walk, I shuffle. I can't hustle like the rest of the runners. The line moves in slowly and now I follow it, having to stand. I shift slowly back and forth from leg to leg. I feel heavy and my head feels the heaviest. It sits on my neck bending it down like an iced tree.

As the lunch orders are given, the line shortens and I move inside, past the refrigerator, then around the column, and then finally to the phones. I hope I don't get a World Trade One or one of the bank orders that are heavy multiple bags and a long walk. I hope I don't get one of the bank orders even though they are the best tips.

The woman has a phone set on so both hands are free. She's scribbling out orders while she hands out the bags. She hands me a bag without looking at me and holds out her hand. I look at the yellow tag on the bag to see how much the lunch is and I pay her up front for the delivery. I get the change together slowly, pulling it out of my pocket and counting it and recounting it, and she becomes impatient and takes my bill and makes change for it in the register. I make my way out of the store sideways. The store is filled now not only with runners who try to flatten against the wall, and around the column, but with the beginning of lunchtime customers.

The delivery is for World Trade Four and that makes me thankful. The World Trade Two building is far, and the World Trade One building is farther still. World Trade Four is only across the street. As I cross the concrete island, a street musician is on it and a small crowd has gathered around him. I pass hearing only a few acoustic chords. I recognize the song but it's dull in my head. Then I hear my name blared above the street musician's song, it's the boss with his electric bullhorn telling me to move. He can see me. I have to react. I push myself, driving my legs, almost to a fast walk until I disappear from his view inside the World Trade Four. Inside, there is a mall and as I enter it the air-conditioning hits me. It almost revives me. The mall is full of lunchtime people. I navigate through them. I go into an elevator. I'm usually alone in the elevators but it is lunch hour and it is packed with people. The chatter is loud and indecipherable. It's a "bad" day in August, the weather is mild, and the throngs move out into the open to get their lunch outdoors, making it a light day for deliveries. A "bad" day is a good day for me. I do less walking.

The elevator opens at the floor I need and I walk slowly but find the room I need quickly because I've been there so many times before. It's a famous room number among the runners because the receptionist there is young and beautiful. I don't have to say anything to her, I don't have to talk. If I could make conversation easily I'd be working on the phones squeezed in the back of the deli and not walking. I put the bag on the desk in front of her with the paper tag that has the extension of the person who ordered the food. She smiles. She always smiles with a perfect set of teeth. I can't smile back. I sit down in the waiting area. I look at my sneakers with my hands clasped between my legs. I'm hunched over and it's only the beginning of lunch.

She calls back to the offices reaching the person who ordered the food. I look at her. She smiles when she is on the phone. Her hand has a flashing engagement ring. Her blouse is clinging and sheer and I can see through her brassiere to her nipple. I feel no admiration or yearning. There's no novelty in this. I don't want her breast. I look at my sneakers again. I only want to sit here.

When it all deserted me, God became "I know I'm not God, but I feel like God, but maybe I am" to "I know I'm not God, but I feel like God," to simply "I feel like God," and then "I feel like God but I'm not." It left altogether and took the racing and the euphoria with it. Sitting in the waiting area, waiting for my money, it all felt opposite to what I felt in January: the particles of the world seemed to have slowed to a stop and rather than being able to stick my finger between the spinning atoms, I was caught in them and they were making my molecules heavier, as if particles had been added and I was heavier than everyone else and I had to drag the extra weight around.

No one has come to pick up the lunch. The receptionist calls back again. I look at my watch. It's been ten
minutes. I should forget about it and take back the
lunch and get on with the rest of the deliveries but instead I zero out looking at the carpet. I'm worried about
the tips I'm missing but I want to kill the lunch hour.
I think, in all the hustle of lunch, no one will know
that I'm missing and when I come back I'll bring the bag
and get a reprimand for being stupid and negligent. I
know I'm missing tips. I'm not making any money. The
thought beats on me and adds to the constant feeling
of tension. The receptionist calls back again. We wait
another ten minutes and then she advises me to take
the lunch back. I should go. I should really go. I shake
my head as though I can't speak English, and she's
happy to go back to her personal phone call.

I zero out looking at my watch. I look at the second
hand which races around the dial and then I look at the
minute hand which nudges itself forward and then I
look at the hour hand which never seems to move. I
feel like an hour hand. I look at the short hour hand,
fixating on it. I'll wait for it. As I wait I hear my mind's
chatter in the background. It's murmuring about tips
and nipples. People pass through the waiting area ig-
noring me. With my head bowed to my wrist I see their
shoes. They ask for any messages and tell the receptionist that they are going out to lunch. I'm a fixture
now, like the plant and the lights. I stick with my wrist-
watch. With my lunch bag and my white T-shirt that
has the delicatessen's name printed on it I have a reason to be here. I know I have no reason to be here. The
customer isn't coming out and it is as if I walked out
of the sun to sit down. I'm loitering and no one is going
to stop me because I have a lunch bag I belong to and

I'm wearing a T-shirt with a delicatessen's name on it.

It's a long time and a short time, both at the same time, until the employees begin to change direction coming in again. I watch their shoes going back in to the offices as they ask for messages. My watch reads one o'clock and then without saying anything to the receptionist I pick up the bag and head back. Walking against the crowd, I feel the dullness of the outside air as I leave the air-conditioning. I cross the street. All the runners are counting their change and comparing tips outside the store. I go in and put the bag on the desk. One of the women on the phone says she'll call the number and find out what happened.

I go outside the store and sit on the fire hydrant until I'm called back in. I think about how I'm not making any money. I'm not making anything. I'm to deliver what is by now a very cold lunch. I take the lunch back to World Trade Four. Lunch hour is over and the mall has fewer people and the elevator is empty. This is futile. This is some kind of punishment. All I want to do is sit and stare at the floor.

I go back to the room with the pretty receptionist and someone must have told the receptionist that her breast was showing through because now she's got her jacket on. She's still smiling. I sit down without even putting the lunch on the desk. She calls back. I feel the pain in my head. I push it down. I zero out again. I stare at the carpet.

No one ever comes to pick up the lunch. I walk back with it like I own it by default. I take it to the woman at the phones and she gives me back the money I paid for the bag. There is no reprimand because the owner is busy arguing with a counterman. I sit on the fire hydrant and look out at the street. The scene is almost in black and white with the sun blaring in like an overexposure. I zero out listening to the Dominican runners chatter away in Spanish. It's all in the background. Everything recedes to the background.

When it's three o'clock and the end of my shift, I've made less than five dollars in tips and that's all from breakfast. That's very bad. I hate myself for it.

The bus I take from Manhattan into Brooklyn stops in front of Trinity Church. That's its second stop. I can walk to the first stop to ensure myself a seat but I'm too tired to guarantee that. I know if there is no seat at Trinity there is no seat for the entire ride, but I walk to the church and lean against a wall waiting for the bus. The pain shoots in and I know how to handle it. I zero out looking at the church graveyard, slumping, getting into the closest sitting position I can standing up. I look at the tombstones but I don't really see them. People pass and they are in the background, the sound of the street mutes. I'm very worried that I won't get a seat. I berate myself for not walking to the first stop. Then the bus is coming, and as it nears I try to see through the windshield how full it is. It's hard to tell. There are people sitting in the front in pairs like they always are. There are always people sitting in the front.

The bus comes and I get on. There is a seat way at the back of the bus where the ventilation system is and I make my way to the back and sit down. The fumes from the back of the bus begin to make me slightly nauseous as the bus moves through the traffic leaving Lower Manhattan. I go back into my trance staring at the aluminum color on the back of the seat in front of me. My eyes narrow. The sun is beating hard through the window and I feel the images come up of the beginning of a dream. Then I fall asleep. When I wake up the bus is in

Brooklyn and the woman next to me is pushing me off
her shoulder. My eyes are dry and there is saliva at the
corners of my mouth. The sunlight bakes me even in an
air-conditioned bus.

My stop comes up and I make my way to the front of
the bus where I stand waiting for the bus to stop. I get
off. I walk home. There's the trudging of a block, the
duplex houses, the streetlights, the stairs and putting
the key into the door and I'm in. I go into my bedroom
and lie down and fall asleep.

When I wake I feel strangely rested. I never feel rested
after I sleep. I sometimes feel more tired. Something is
different. I can feel it. I slept only an hour but the light
feels different. It feels soft. I rub my hand over my face
and feel the texture of my hand on my face. I look up
at the ceiling. It doesn't seem as imposing as it usually
does. I must have dreamed about school because I have
the word *September* in my head. It rings in my head
with all the references of fall: brown and red leaves,
notebooks, light jackets, school. I look at the wall. There
is a poster there. It's a painting by Gauguin of a Tahi-
tian woman. The composition is purple and orange. All
summer I've zeroed out looking at that poster. It said
nothing to me. It was only a shape to put into the background while I tried to think of nothing. Now it has
something. I can see the purple. I can see the richness
and intensity of the purple of the woman's gown. It
has nuance. Something is different. Something has
changed. I'm thinking about school in the fall and I feel
positive: brown and red leaves, notebooks, light jackets,
school. I can see myself outside of Shimkin Hall waiting
for a class, near Washington Square Park where the
leaves are turning brown and red.

It's over. It's over.

What happened? Was it the sleep? Was it the medication finally working? I think about the poster. The purple. I admire it. I feel appreciation for it. I appreciate it. That's the key. It's a matter of appreciation. It's a matter of will. Appreciate. I go into the living room and turn on the stereo to hear the music. I hear it. I hear every note. The bass. The treble. I follow the lyrics and notes. I get involved with it. I sing to a song I know. I can feel energy, but I feel a relaxation I haven't felt in a long time. I sit in the living room chair with my head up, not bowed, so I can see through the window. There are children playing ball outside against the stoop across the street and I can hear them and see them and their animation doesn't make me feel jealous and sad. I don't feel tense and tight like before. I don't feel screwed up inside and ready to explode. I can breathe again. I promise myself that tomorrow I'll make twenty-five dollars in tips. I continue to look out the window. The sun seems friendly and the sky is pastel. I appreciate it. I want to tell someone. I want to tell someone that it is over. I go back into the bedroom and go through my address book. I'm looking for someone to talk with. I find a name and call it but no one's home. I look at my watch. It's seven o'clock. I'll wait, I'll wait until everyone's home and I'll talk on the phone all night.

I'm hungry now. I go to the kitchen and in the refrigerator are some leftovers from last night's dinner. I'm ravenous. It tastes wonderful, and it's like I haven't really eaten in a long time. What to do now? I clean up the plates, forks, and aluminum foil and sit back down in the living room. The sun is beginning to set and it looks bloodred in the sky. That means it will be a hot day tomorrow. A "good" day. I'll make twenty dollars in tips easily.

September.

In September I'll be going back to film school. My mind wanders as the shadows begin to move into the room. I look at the carpet but while I'm watching the flecks of sunlight on the carpet I'm not blocking, I'm not thinking of nothing or zeroing out, I'm thinking of the receptionist and her image makes a warmth in my head. It clears my head, and I keep her in my head as I feel the warmth and lucidity spread. This is a renaissance. It's over. It's over.

I shift my stare up from the carpet to the table following the sunlight as it gleams against the finished wood and then up to the base of the lamp where it hugs the chrome. The shadows are moving in and the furniture is slowly getting swallowed up and I can see it.

Renaissance. Renaissance? Nipples. Tips. You won't ever make up the tips you've lost all summer. You'll never make up those tips if you have a week of twenty-dollar days.

The room is going dark now and losing its color. The thought of never making up the summer expands like a disease and I feel the tightness in my head and stomach again. It grows and I slouch in my chair.

How will you face September? How can you count on yourself to be competent?

The room slows into darkness and the gleam on the table and the sunlight on the chrome disappear and everything is brown and gray. The music has become loud and annoying, and I lower it and then I shut it off. Got to get to bed. The pressure is back and it beats at my forehead like a hammer. My mouth has dried. It seems a long way from the living room chair to the bedroom. I have to measure my progress as I do on the street. I have to cite landmarks. Dining room. I move through it. Front door. I move past it. Refrigerator. I go by it, and then there is the bedroom. I drop onto the bed and cover myself with the blanket. I listen to the chirp of the birds outside. I open my eyes under the blankets. The room is almost dark and under the blankets it is pitch black.

Appreciate.

I pull off the blanket slowly and look at the Gauguin poster as if it were some monster behind a locked door. The purple has no life to it. The woman who before seemed to have some optimism has none now. Her purple turns brown, then black as she is swallowed up in the darkness. I look up at the ceiling which seems to be lowering on me, and I stare at it, blocking and zeroing out.

There is nothing here except the emptiness with a for-ever receding horizon. The sky is lifeless like glass with nothing behind it.

The phone rings. I let it go. I won't pick it up. I haven't used it, except for this afternoon, in a very long time and I won't be using it again.

I have to get up. This will take only a little energy and a little time and then it will be all over. I get up, dredging my weight up as if it were sea wreckage, and go to the closet. I go into the closet and take out my belt, and pushing myself forward with the belief that I have a cure, I go into the living room where the hanging plant is hooked to the ceiling.

I take the plant off the hook and put it on the floor. I strap the belt tightly around my neck and hook the strap end to the plant hook. Then I kneel and I bring one leg out. Then I lie down with my neck craned forward so that the strap still has some slack. When I ease the muscles in my neck the belt should choke. I block out all resistance, all the good things, and all the fear and let my head relax back with my eyes shut.

My head hits the carpet and there's a pop from above and the hook lands on my chest. I lie there for a while. I look at my watch. Someone will be home soon and they can't see me like this. I stick the hook back in the ceiling and hang the plant on it, and then completely defeated I trudge back to the bedroom where I hide under the covers again.

Dining room. Door. Bedroom. The birds have stopped chirping and there's only the sound of far-off cars. I can hear keys at the front door and then I can hear the door open. There are steps on the kitchen floor, and my bedroom door creaks open. It's my mother checking on me. I zero out under the blanket. There are levels in this nothingness. I approach each level leaving something behind, erasing something. At the top is September, it shrivels away like fall, then there is the lady receptionist, a nipple is only what it is and even less than that. I know tomorrow I will have to wake up and face another day of running and I feel unhappy but I let that go. It doesn't matter. I disappear. Somehow I make it happen. I don't care and tomorrow disappears. I feel my own breath in my face. It gets slower and fat with dampness. I breathe heavily and rhythmically pretending I'm asleep and soon I am. The last thing I hear are the sounds of my mother in the kitchen, and the last thing I think of is September and how everything was going to be fine.

## WINTER 1985

I'm walking along the outskirts of Washington Square Park thinking how the winter is a good time for Judgment Day. This winter. Now. The texts must be revised. The lights burn in the lamps along the park and I know they're not burning electricity anymore. They are powered by sound, and to usher in the Messianic Age there will be a couple, a courtship, a man and woman.

I'm walking through the street with Corey.

I want to tell her.

I want to tell her who I am and what I've been through but I wonder if she's ready yet. I'll try to make it a joke somehow, no, I'll tell her straight out in the coffee shop. How shall I start? That I am God and she is my avatar?

We're having coffee and she's telling me about her family and work at the library and school. She doesn't like working the desk at the library very much but it's better than working in the stacks. All I can think of is how I can introduce myself and I don't see how I can and suddenly I become the reformed criminal—there's nothing abnormal with me. I don't need to say anything.

When we're finished at the coffee shop she kisses me and I go home elated, and I'm God and I'm on the L train intoxicated with the thought that this is it. THIS IS IT.

The days go very easily now, and schoolwork goes smoothly as well. I work by the light box making my sketches thinking of how I have truly received absolution. I have what I want. Things look good for a change.

I pick up Corey at her dorm room and we go see *Citizen Kane* at a revival cinema and the film goes by very fast and every frame in the film is full of a secret language of metaphors. After we go to a restaurant, I bring her back to her dorm room and she invites me in. Her roommate is out and it's the two of us alone. She has three metal balls hanging over the bed. I ask why and she says that they are pawn shop balls. She says that she likes kitsch items and antiques, the more unintentionally ironic the better. She says she's hoping to get a lawn jockey or a pink flamingo so she can bring it with her when she goes home for good in the summer. Only I know there will be no more seasons after this one. I kiss her under the pawn balls like they were mistletoe. We sit down on the bed and I begin to unbutton her shirt and she pulls back. So I let it go. We just kiss and I think next time.

I think of Corey all the time, her face fills my head.

We go to a movie, a restaurant, her roommate is again away for the weekend and she pulls back at my unbuttoning her shirt. She won't even let me feel her breasts. I go out with Corey to the same coffee shop and we talk and then go back to her room. We kiss. I move my hands toward her breasts and she pulls them away. She puts my hand on her crotch. I rub her hand and then I open the pants and move up to the breasts again, and she pulls my hands away and opens my fly.

In the dark, careful not to move into her nonerogenous zone, we make love with her shirt on like a life jacket. I go home on the train feeling invincible with the weight of these events.

It's Christmas time, and lights are hung throughout the streets of Brooklyn and when I commute home to Canarsie from Manhattan I feel the celebration of the lights. I want to get Corey a gift, a return of the Magi, something ironic and kitschy and in my price range. I look in the art galleries in the Village and there are a lot of things with potential but everything is too expensive. Where do I get a lawn jockey or a pink flamingo in Lower Manhattan? I sit in the lounge of the first floor of the Loeb Student Center, sinking into my seat in deep thought, whispering "frankincense and myrrh" to myself, and just as I can't remember the third gift I don't know where to go in the city to get what I need. I even think of going on the Long Island Railroad and going from house to house, lawn to lawn, in an effort to filch a lawn jockey when it hits me—I'm thinking too much, go out of this building and the gift will find you. It's here. It's nearby. It's within walking distance. I can feel it calling me and I know that all I have to do is follow the signs.

Flying out the doors of the student center I go to the nearest corner, which is Washington Square South and right off the park, because the gift is near. The sign says one way and although I know this is for moving traffic I also know this is a secret message for me to go the way the sign is pointing. I walk up Washington Square South along the park, past Bobst Library where I met Corey (which is a good omen) until Washington Square South turns into West 4th Street and for a moment I hesitate not knowing what to do, but then I know to go right but there is no right, only the library, which forces me left and I damn the library and every book in it and keep walking along the park on Washington Square East.

Now it occurs to me that if I keep going left, which is the devil's way, that I'll go around and around the park, so I break this trap by going right, which is the way of God. I turn onto Washington Place sneaking through the big hips of NYU—the main building and the bookstore—and now I'm home free and reveling in the passion of my mission until I reach the dead end of Broadway. There up ahead of me beckoning me in, swallowing me whole, is the Unique Clothing Shop and I cross the street and go in even though I would bet I will find nothing antique or ironic in there.

I go directly to a floor person and ask if there's anything antique in the store to which she immediately responds that I should try the Antique Boutique right next door. I'm overwhelmed and I thank her and make a mental note of her name, which is Natalie, as it says on her blouse.

When I get inside the Antique Boutique I'm crestfallen—there's nothing but jackets and shirts. Even in my grief and disappointment I can't help but put down a few deposits which I never plan to pick up. Now I'm on Broadway again going right, and I've diminished the money in my wallet which was all I had in my bank account. It was supposed to be for Corey.

How could I have gone wrong? Even the colors that showed the way were right—the flapping violet banners of NYU. Purple is always good for me.

I go right until I reach Astor Place and then I go right again because right is right and God's way, and I see it in the distance, the big cube sculpture, resting on one edge like an impossible die, and as big as a house, sitting where Lafayette meets Astor. THIS IS A MANHATTAN LAWN JOCKEY!!! I stand by it enjoying it until I become very sad with the realization that I can't give it to Corey. Then the wind picks up and I put my hands in my pockets, still transfixed by the sculpture, and it comes down to me like the saddest epiphany, a tragic one—the best things belong to everyone.

It begins to snow and I leave the cube behind. I walk, dejected, through the beginnings of the sticking snow and I know I'm going east but I don't know where. I go east looking in store windows thinking about changing my gift goals, and as I do this, as I compromise, I feel that I'm compromising Corey and it feels as though everything I felt was right and my belief that a gift was waiting for me falls down. It falls down like a wall around me, brick by brick, and turns into snow. I'm still moving east and almost tearful when I come to a Spanish store that sells religious items, a botanica.

I go inside and the place smells of fragrant candles burning. I look around and there are rosary beads and saint medallions in little plastic packages and I think this is home. I was directed here. Behind the counter is a little man with glasses who is looking at me as if he's certain that I am in the wrong place. On the wall is a clock made of Christ on the cross with his right arm as an hour hand and his left as a minute hand while a thin red second hand goes around him. He is in relief with his crown of thorns and trickles of painted blood are under it and behind him is a stained glass window design in blue and gold. It has the harvest seasons delineated. It looks plastic and that's perfect.

I ask the man behind the counter how much he wants for the clock. He says in broken English that it is not for sale. If only he knew who I was, that clock belongs to me. I offer him everything I have for the clock. He answers that the clock has been in the store for cinco años. I offer it to him again. He takes the clock off the wall and says that he can't wrap it and he doesn't have the box to put it in. I tell him not to wrap it, I'll just take it.

Now I make my way through the maze of the East Side until I find a subway station and I get on the platform with my clock under my arm, cord dangling, and my thoughts are clipping along—where was I five years ago when this clock first went up on the botanica wall? I was in high school. Looseleafs. Crushes. First sex. Breasts. I think of Corey with her hidden breasts and then back to the clock again. What's a clock say? Now. Now. Again and again. And when should I be giving this present to Corey—Now! Now!

The train comes down the track but I don't get on. I go back upstairs and walk west following an invisible sun as the snow makes a solid gray sheet of everything. I'm happy now. I'm on a mission again and I've got everything I need. Before I know it I'm back to Astor Place and I give the cube a pat, going by. Broadway. Washington Place. The violet banners, they're with me now. The park. Corey's dorm is right off the park, not far from the student center. I go in and sit down in her lounge only now realizing how cold I am.

I get up and go to her room which is at the end of the hall right off the lounge. I'm smiling and I knock. There is no answer. She could be in the shower. She could be in class. Where could she be? I'm determined to sit in the lounge and wait for her with my eyes trained on the front door. By the door is a Christmas tree with streamers and lights and a Star of Bethlehem on the top. I look at the Christ on my clock. There is no Christ without a tragedy, so why does everything seem like a party to me? I look at my watch. That's one revelation. I'll time them as they come, like a woman in labor, to pass the waiting.

Where is Corey?

If I come unexpected to a place, shouldn't I really be expected? That is, if I'm in tune with everything, shouldn't wherever I am be the right place to be? If I am truly what I believe I am, then the answer is yes. That is why I keep missing classes and everything is still fine and that is why I put off my schoolwork till later, because there is no later, there is only now. If Corey is what I believe her to be, then she'd know that and know I was coming and be here for me.

Where is Corey?

Then after ten minutes that hang like a week with nothing to do, after six revelations, just like a cavalry officer she walks through the door to save me. She's covered with snow and she doesn't see me. She doesn't look into the lounge and walks through the outer hallway heading for her room.

I give it a moment, a beat, to keep the effect of randomness and then I go back there for our surprise meeting. I prop the clock against the wall and knock on the door. She asks who it is. I tell her and she opens the door.

She is surprised, a little taken aback, and her smile is slightly tense. Am I not wanted? Could this have been all wrong? Could I have read every sign to a wrong conclusion? She says that she just came from a bitch of an exam and she's bummed out. I want to tell her that it doesn't matter, that nothing matters, but I can't, I can't compose it in my head in a way that leaves out everything I know about who I am and that at this point would all be too much for Corey. I just hug her and when we pull apart I put up my finger as if to say one minute and I go to the door and open it to pull in the clock. A big smile crosses her face. She laughs and kisses me. Then she leans it against her roommate's bed and the wall so we can see it. We shut off the lights and plug it in and it glows in the dark. We lie back down on her bed together with our clothes still a little wet from the snow and the clock is like a kitsch fireplace. Everything feels at peace for a while. I can feel the thoughts in my head slowing, going from a river to a brook.

Then Corey gets up and goes into the bathroom. I can hear her taking off her wet clothes. She comes out and stands by the bathroom. She's backlit by the bathroom light. She's nude from the waist down. Her pubic hair is dark and her legs are long and beautiful. She's still wearing the shirt like a life jacket. Suddenly I feel incredibly ashamed, ashamed that I let it go this far without telling her and I begin to say I'm God but I don't finish it that way because I say I'm a manic-depressive. Her face becomes very still, and she's wearing those listening eyes, and I know I have to explain what I've said although I know full well that a manic-depressive is not exactly what I am, that would make everything a disease and not a transformation which I know it has to be, proven it to be. I tell her that I have highs and lows, that I'm moody, that I've been in a hospital for it, knowing this is an old script, a script that belongs to someone else now. She looks at me and for a moment I don't know what she's thinking and what she's going to say, and then she says that she's been hiding a secret from me too and she unbuttons her shirt and unhooks her bra. I had always suspected up until that moment that it was a matter of tenderness, or one breast being too large, and even that there was some secret message there for me. Padding spills out of the left cup. Her left breast is not there. There is just smooth skin and the tiniest of scars. I want to run. Then she tells me about it, the surgery, everything, and my response is to let everything go—the minutiae, it's not enough just to say the label but it's only enough to describe the whole thing, the Arts Building, the bus ride to college, the phone call from my mother, the devil in the refrigerator, the devil in the hospital, going to New Jersey, the mail room, the Born Again Christians, the trains, the miles and miles of train rides. It's like making love with grief.

After everything is expelled we know the best thing is that it's all over. The worst, that is, and we feel better and make love in the dark completely nude, both of us, in the ticking glow of the Jesus clock.

## SUMMER 1986

The train pulls into the station. I make it solid with two different shades of gray. The people that exit—each one has a hair and coat color that separates them from the figure alongside. I practice my typing speed for an hour. I write with difficulty, pausing, brainstorming, staring at the page, producing a line at a time until after three hours I have half a page of dialogue. The characters are not developed, they hang on lines. The play is too short, not long enough to be full-length, only the scope of a one-act. I'll try again tomorrow.

The people are big in the frame. You can see their faces now. I color their skin with flesh tone. I type but this time only a half hour before I lose concentration. I'm going backwards, losing lines that seem wrong now and putting them back and losing them again. I sit in concentrated indecision. The brainstorming perpetuates itself. It circles. The tension continues, I take it with me after I've left the table, after writing nothing. Then I come back to stare at the page, repeating the same list of possible ideas, stop, and come back again. Perhaps it will be better tomorrow.

The pencils are continually dulling and chipping. Instead of slowing down, I speed up in a cursory manner. The lines are bad, slashes and tracks. I can't work as long as I usually do, the way I did when I was doing the initial drawings—four hours, five hours at the light box. Now I stop after half an hour. I set up for typing. I type five minutes. I set up for writing. I write nothing. I sit on the couch with my hands clasped and the TV off watching the clock under the lamp just to fix my eyes on something other than lined paper, but the concentrated effort continues. There is the day left, and I've used up all my things to do. I can't stop thinking. Tomorrow then.

I take out the drawings and then put them away. I can't type. I stare at the empty page. The day is over at ten o'clock in the morning. I don't even count the hours left because if I stay awake unable to sleep, they're more. I sit on the couch with my hands clasped and the TV off watching the clock. Ten five. Ten six. Ten seven. I close my eyes and pray the half hour will pass when I open them. Ten eight. Ten nine. I'm not hungry at twelve even though a meal would be an event that could space out the day. I don't eat or smoke. My only activity is staring and thinking, but my thought is not about the play although that returns. The thought drops out leaving only the tension and the feeling of an iron hat on my head. I want to lie down in bed, but it's the middle of the day. I keep myself from going into the bedroom to the bed. Three days from now I have a job interview. It is as if I'm in a waiting room waiting for it.

I take out the drawings and sit in front of them, and then put them away. I take out the typewriter and put it back. I stare at the page. I sit on the couch with my hands clasped and the TV off watching the clock. I turn on the TV but I can't concentrate on it. I think of music. I can't listen to music. I can't eat. I can't smoke. I keep myself from going to bed but it's hard. I think about starting the day again: taking out the drawings and sitting in front of them, and then putting them away. Take out the typewriter and then put it back. Stare at the page just to keep from lying down. Tomorrow will be the same as today and I'm scared of the page and I'm scared of facing the bed in the daytime.

I stare at the page. I sit on the couch with my hands clasped. I get up. I go to bed. I lie down in bed but I can't sleep. I sit on the couch with my hands clasped. I go back to the bedroom. In the dark room I stare at the ceiling. Lying in one position on my back with my body not needing sleep, the pillow begins to get damp under my head, my hands begin to get pins and needles. I have to shift my position. I can look at the ceiling. I can look at the shade. I can look at the clock. No sleep to cancel it with. Although I close my eyes there is no getting there. My mouth tastes horrible from not eating. I'm not hungry. I might go into the kitchen and get some juice and then come back to bed. My head hurts. It's in a holding pattern, one thought. When I get up it's to go into the bathroom and throw up the pills. I look in the mirror at myself, the amount of Haldol I tried to overdose with has made black circles under my eyes. When my brother comes home from work he finds me in bed with the shades down. I tell him I'm going back to the hospital. I can't trust myself any longer. I went to the job interview in Manhattan, arriving very early. It was near Washington Square Park, near the NYU student activity building. I went up to the comedy magazine office, and I was so drawn to the window that I had to rush back downstairs to save myself, as if the height was a willing accomplice and I sat in Washington Square Park, where it was ground level, and safe, staring into space. Staring at the people. Lying in bed, I look at the ceiling. My head hurts. The iron hat. The next room is my mother's bedroom, and there is a screen door that leads to a back porch. A willing accomplice one story high. It will be like drowning in a thimble of water. I walk to the back porch like a sleepwalker and lean against the rail. My brother, who has just gotten off the phone with my mother who is visiting in California, comes out to the porch and holds me by the shoulder leading me back inside. Deciding to go back to the hospital is at first a liberation. I know I am beyond trusting. I need someone to protect me. I have to shift my position. I have to move my hands. I look at the clock. It's too late. Three days ago I shuttled from staring at the bedroom clock to staring at the living room clock. I went back and forth all day. Sometimes in less than five-minute shifts. It was my activity. Now my shifting of position has narrowed to moving between alternate sides of the bed. The shade. The clock. The ceiling. My brother pulls me away from the rail again, I can't put up a fight. He puts me back in bed and returns to the Giants preseason football game on television. He can't tie me down. He'd have to sit with me all night to stop me, a suicide watch. I stretch out on the bed, face against the pillow staring at the shade in the dark. I go back again. Making it over. Making it stop. There are too many hours to face with nothing to fill them with, and nothing to break them up, and nothing to stop what's happened to the world, and time, and the calendar which is meaningless without events to delineate it. Because I can't participate in the events, and I can't tell anyone because I've lost the power to express it, and I can't relax it away because tension and apprehension are its features, and I can't think it away because thinking is the problem, and I can't will myself through it because it robs the will, and I can't distance myself from it or shut it off. Hoping for a one-story reprieve, putting my waist against the rail, I lean in, almost going to sleep standing up, and fall like a cut tree off the porch. . . .

Loops. I think them, while I lay in bed in Downstate Hospital staring at the ceiling, while I go from my room to the kitchen, to the day room, and back to my room unable to make conversation. They interrupt my thought while I sit in front of my team psychologist and I am barely able to answer him. My mother visits, sitting in a chair while I lie in bed with my clothes on in the dark. I just want something to drink. I'm always thirsty. I've lost the will to eat and smoke. I want juice or soda. She brings sandwiches I won't eat. There is never anything for me to talk about and sometimes she talks about what went on at home. Sometimes it is more than having nothing to talk about, it is about not being able to form sentences. It is almost as if there seemed to be no reason to talk and so I lose my power of speech, and then it comes back. It is a protest that no one pays attention to.

We're in a bright white cubicle, and now that I have my glasses back I can see him. Even as close as a few feet away I was barely able to see my psychologist's features, his eyes. I wasn't allowed to wear my glasses until the surgery on the damage to my eye socket was healed. It was the only injury from the fall even though I was knocked unconscious.

He's asking me to describe what I'm going through. I stop more than pausing, the loop comes through, I can't explain, and there's a silence before I can answer. I say I don't know how I feel.

My mother comes to pick me up for a weekend pass and I confess I want to die. I'm thinking of killing myself. If you take me home I will go to the train station. I had thought about it. The Rockaway Parkway station is the last stop on the line and the train would come in too slow and so I'd have to take the train one stop up the line to New Lots and do it there. I didn't want to. Like a curtain coming down a nurse appears sitting at the door and my pass is canceled. One-on-one suicide watch. I don't speak to the nurse like some patients, I can't. I lie in bed. I sit up. I lie in bed. I drink the juice my mother leaves me, boxes of juice with straws. I stand at the doorway, at its invisible barrier, and look down the hall. The nurse is called away for a moment and I walk out, heading for the door to the ward. My room is at the front of the ward, and the door, which is usually electronically closed, is open, and I walk out waiting for the elevator when a hand grabs me and pulls at my arm. It's one of the nurses, and I don't fight back, and they put me back in my room and take away my shoes. The nurse's reaction is that she could have lost her job on that move, and mother's reaction when she is told of my aborted elopement is to ask where I would go. She is incredulous. I lie in bed. I sit up. I stare at the wall. I lie at night listening for the blood pressure machine on wheels that they bring around at five, and I know I have not slept again for a whole night. There isn't a clock here to watch. The window is behind me. There is the wall, the ceiling and my roommate, who sleeps all day unless they drag him out to meetings. The loops never stop and the tension never decreases.

There is a problem. If I'm not suicidal and I'm not feeling suicidal, then I say I'm not suicidal. If I am suicidal but I want to live, then I say I am suicidal, but if I am suicidal and making plans—which is the true test of being suicidal—then I say I'm not suicidal because I am severely suicidal and want to get out so I can accomplish it.

On pass at home I lie in bed for eight hours eyes open thinking about the Drano under the sink and how I can get myself to use it. I want no pain and that is the hard part about Drano, it would be a lot of pain. I remember someone telling me about the time they saw a man jump onto the tracks, that it cut the poor bastard's head right off. It seemed like it would happen in an instant and be over, a modern guillotine. I try escaping from the house, but blocking the hallway, my mother slaps me and my brother holds me, screaming that I can't leave the house. On the way back to the hospital I try to stop the steering wheel because I don't want to go back, they aren't helping me, I can't kill myself in there.

When I give the news to myself that I am going to die it is both a sentence and a reprieve. Death becomes the new anxiety. It is its own loop: I have to kill myself because I can't stand the panic, which then becomes I feel panic because I'm going to kill myself. I calm myself for a moment with the thought that I don't have to kill myself and then the panic returns. In the end it becomes the cure, task, goal. It is like taking castor oil. The key is not to think about it. Heights scare me more than trains, even if the result is the same. It is just a few feet from the platform to the tracks. The heights make me think more about the fact that I am dying, and roofs are less accessible than stations.

I didn't know I had the privilege until the end of the first day it is given to me. I am permitted to go out with a fellow patient for half an hour once a shift. I decide the night before what I will do. I persuade a patient to accompany me. He knows the neighborhood better than I do. I ask him if he can show me where the subway is because I am planning on a pass to go to Manhattan. It is a lie and I know he knows it is a lie. He lets me off at the station closest to Downstate. I tell him I am going to NYU. I know I can't accomplish immediately what I intend to, that it will take some time, and so I take the first train to another station so they won't find me at the station. I loiter. I get on trains that can do the job going from station to station.

I'm thirsty but why drink when I'm going to die? I go upstairs to the street and get a can of soda anyway. It is bright, a very hot late September day. I go back down into the station because I started this and have to finish it. A cop yells from a distance that I should wait on the middle of the platform and not near the tunnel, and I comply. A train comes in. It's slow. It creeps through the tunnel. It won't do. The station is beginning to fill with people. I wait with them. Making this train means more for me than their separate destinations. The lights of a train are coming through the tunnel. I see the cop coming back from behind me. He knows.

Now!

There is a blank, as though I've succeeded in erasing consciousness as I hoped to, and then there is machinery. The sky in heaven is made of metal parts. No. It's the train. I'm on my back on the tracks looking at the underbelly of the 2 train. I twist my head to see my arm lying on the tracks a few feet in front of me. It still has the denim sleeve on it. My left arm is tucked underneath me, and I pull it out to touch my right shoulder which is wet with blood.

I scream. I introduce myself to the crowd on the platform as if I am placing a 911 call to them. A woman on the platform yells that they're coming to help me. She's kind. I am sure most of the commuters on the platform are annoyed. Not to mention the people in the train.

I'm thirsty. Terribly thirsty. In front of me is a dirty pool of water. I bend my neck down to it like dogs do.

The paramedic asks if I can move my foot. I can't and I tell him. My other foot is touching the rail and is burnt through the sneaker.

They'll sew back my arm. They will.

I hear them say they are going to use air bags to lift the train, and they say not to look at the arm. But I've been looking at the arm the whole time. I am freed from beneath the wheel and put on a stretcher. I see faces. I see the cop who had been running toward me. Helicopter sounds. A voice says he had to get all wet down there.

Put me out. Put me out. That's what I've wanted from the very beginning. When they are putting me through the CAT scan I am still pleading with them to put me out.

The nurses washing me in the ICU hurt me. I ask them to stop, but they say I did this to myself.

I'm on so much morphine that I usually don't know where I am. I'm in my grandmother's house with a big mirror in front of me and I ask the nurse to unball my fist, only for her to find that I have no arm. I have new loops to contend with about no right arm and no right leg. My doctor wants me to get into the wheelchair and I refuse so they forcibly put me in and wheel me half naked up and down the hallway, and they're laughing. I refuse to go back in the wheelchair and I speak into the intercom alongside the rail of my bed continually calling the night staff, crying to them that I want my arm and leg back. With the criblike situation I'm in, the bedpan under me, the catheter in me, I fling my shit at the wall. I expose myself to the psychiatrist who comes to visit me. I lie mute. I babble. I threaten to try to get off the bed thinking I can somehow get to the window hopping on my one casted leg and get myself out. My father comes in and goes berserk on the nurse so badly that they threaten to call security. When I arrive in Trauma on the tenth floor I become fully aware of how badly I am injured. I have a cast on my left leg. My right leg has been amputated below the knee. My head is shaved and bandaged. My right arm is gone. There are two fiercely red patches where the skin has been removed to be grafted on the heel and side of the left foot. My back is bandaged.

The window seems far from the bed although it's no more than four feet away. If I could crawl there without the nurses seeing me and climb up to the ledge, I'd crawl out. It's dark now and the lights are out on the ward. A nurse sits in a chair outside my room and they've taken my intercom away. Hearing a commotion in my room, the nurse comes in to find me contorted in my sheets. He asks me what I'm doing but I'm beyond a reply. Telling him would ruin my strategy of trying to hang myself in the cavelike dark, in my bedsheets.

## WINTER 1987

The sun is bright coming through the window. I've been sleeping on and off, going back to my dream of running, and listening to the nurses speak in low tones about a European vacation. They're sitting at the foot of the bed on a double suicide watch. One for me and one for my roommate, whom I've never been introduced to.

The nurses go on vacation. They talk about expenses. This is what people do. People wear clothes. They change them every day. They come to work. They go home. This is what people do. This is what they do. People wear clothes. They change them every day. They come to work. They work, they go home. There is a difference between day and night and morning and noon and breakfast and lunch. And if there is not, at least a vacation would make them happy. Money means something because it can make them happy.

I can't write because I have no hand to write. I can't draw because I have no hand to draw. I can't get out of bed because I have one leg in a cast and one leg chopped off, and even with all this it is the same. I lie back on the pillow and stare at the ceiling. The ceiling. The window. My roommate. I listen to the nurses talk about their vacation. I feel tense but I don't move. The tension is deep down. On the surface I am numb. I feel nothing. The sun makes it hard to sleep. It makes the sheet warm. It makes it hard to go away and to forget. I close my eyes and try to ignore it, turning my face into the pillow.

I don't have an arm. I don't have a leg. I can't walk. I hear this over and over in my head. I hate myself in my head but everywhere else I feel nothing. It is as if I were paralyzed, and not an amputee. The world is the room. The nurses. The food tray. My roommate. The ceiling. The world ends at the doorway where flashes of people pass and begins at the window where the sun comes in. Slitting my eyes to the sunlight I look between the nurses at the rolling table that brings the trays. It's not noon. I know because I still see the oatmeal and the milk container of the breakfast tray I haven't touched. Push on. Squeeze as much sleep out of the morning as you can. The afternoon is for thinking about the leg and the arm.

I close my eyes again. I can hear noises outside the door—footsteps, wheels. Then I go back to my dream of running in the hot sunlight. Someone outside calls "lunch" and I wake, the sound of footsteps outside. I go back to jumping hurdles in my dream. When I finally come up, a lunch tray has replaced the breakfast tray. I can't eat. I can't sleep anymore. I follow the dust in the sunlight with my eyes as it dances over my bed.

I don't have an arm. I don't have a leg. I don't have an arm. I don't have a leg. An arm. A leg. I play with the fingers on my hand trying to remove the dirt from underneath the nails with my thumb. I pick the crusty skin off my casted leg. I hear loud cursing through the wall and I know there is a man in the next room who curses loudly.

A nurse comes in who asks me if I know how long I've been in bed. I don't know. I don't know what day it is. I don't know when I entered the hospital. She asks if I know where I am. I say in the hospital. She says that it's time I move out of the room. It's time I learn where I am.

It takes four nurses to lift me into the wheelchair. It isn't the little Filipino nurses who converse in Tagalog all day outside and give me my treatment, but the taller nurses, the black nurses that put me in. Coming out of the bed I feel the measurements and perspective of the room swirl, the rolling table becomes level to my eyes and close by, the window becomes far away, the door-way, which always seemed to be the beginning of an-other place, is closer now. It seems like a doorway. I'm lower than everything, lower than I was in the raised bed. I feel dizzy. I don't want to leave. I don't fight. They heave me up like a couch and dump me in the wheel-chair, binding me to it with a sheet. It's an old wooden wheelchair, and without an operable foot I can drive it only with my left hand. The nurses leave me. I sit in this new perspective of the room. The ceiling is higher. The walls seem closer. I sit for a while putting my new per-spective into the background while I'm thinking. While I'm blocking. I don't want to go into the hallway, but the room has become tedious and I need new things to block out the inside of my head. I move toward the door, pushing the wheel, rotating the wheel slowly, ever so slowly, like a new student driver, and I get out the door. In the hall I don't get far. Only being able to direct my-self with one hand I go in slow, unsure circles. Unable to direct myself they station me in front of the door to my room like an invalid palace guard.

I am in the hallway, a corridor with rooms adjunct to it. In the foreground a woman lies on the floor against the wall propped on her arms as if she were lying out in a field. She looks as if she's looking at me, but she's not, she's looking through me with faraway eyes to the end of the hall. She's wearing thin blue pajamas that have the printed word BELLEVUE all over them and the soles of her feet are black with floor dirt. She doesn't move. Not even to blink.

Halfway down the hall is a man sitting in a wooden wheelchair against the wall. He's opposite a speaker that's playing soft Muzak. His head is bobbing to the music while he plays with his thumbs and kicks back and forth with one foot. The other leg is amputated.

Beyond him is a man who is standing, leaning like a question mark in the narrow hallway. He seems to be tottering on the brink of falling over and doing a somersault but he just leans, with his head almost to his knees. Nurses pass back and forth under the fluorescence and they disappear into a brightly lit station with big windows. I can hear them talking but it recedes into the station and loses meaning against the Muzak coming from the hall speaker.

A patient comes down the hall. He is well groomed and bearded and walks quickly, stopping in front of me. He introduces himself and begins to ask me questions. What's my name? How did I get here? Do I want to go to the dayroom? I nod although it doesn't matter to me and if nothing matters it doesn't matter if I'm in front of my room or in the dayroom or anywhere.

He gets behind my wheelchair and begins to push. Now the leg of the woman on the floor is in the way and he asks her to move. She doesn't. I think she must be catatonic, but he says he's going to get a nurse and, as if it were on a hinge, the foot retreats. Nothing else on her body moves, not even her eyes, and the foot with the dirty sole moves only enough to let us through. No more, no less.

Passing the man in the wheelchair, my driver loses control momentarily and we swerve into the placid man who, at being bumped, suddenly begins to scream garbled words very angrily and kick at me with his one foot. My driver says he's sorry and moves me on. The leaner stands like a badly cast statue and we move around him and my driver says hi to him. He doesn't respond, only getting deeper into his lean. Now we've reached the end of the hall. My driver says this is the dayroom. It's stark and smoke-filled, and cigarette butts cover the floor. A patient picks one up and puts it in his mouth. There are patients congregated in the dayroom. Talking. Smoking. There is a television suspended high up on the wall. It has a talk show on and no one is watching. There are two big windows that lead out to sunlight that makes shapes on the floor and walls.

I'm pushed near a circle of three patients all in blue pajamas. One is black and has glasses on and is talking about one of the nurses, and there is a white woman in a wheelchair and a Hispanic man wearing a paper mask. I listen to the chatter, using it as a buffer against my head and I look out of the window.

I lie in bed now. There's no longer a nurse in the room. I'm off suicide watch. Now there is no more nurses' chatter about vacations to put in the background while I listen to my head. There's the wall, which has been covered with get-well cards, the ceiling, the window, the sun. I look up at the ceiling. The sun is on my face. The sheets are white and clean. They've just been changed while I was getting breakfast in the day-room. I play with my fingers.

My father is sitting across from me, at the foot of the bed. He asks me if I wrote in the notebook he got me to practice my penmanship. I say no. We both look out the window. We sit in silence while the noises filter in from the hallway and then there is a knock at the open door.

A woman comes in dressed in white pants and announces herself as the physical therapist and tells us that now that I have had my cast removed I will be going downstairs for physical therapy. My father is elated. He wants to know when I'll be going, when I'll get my leg, when I'll be walking. The therapist tries to answer as best she can but I can see she really can't answer questions other than that I will be going to therapy. I have no reaction. I look out the window.

I'm in a big room now, the size of a small gymnasium. The ceiling is bright with fluorescent light and there are big windows overlooking a scenic view of the FDR Highway and the East River. Cars are passing in long lines going up Manhattan. I watch them, the sun glaring like headlights off their windshields. I put them inside my head to block the thoughts of my arm and leg and my constant feeling of wanting to die. I shift my gaze to the near end of the room where there is a wall-length mirror that has a white stationary bicycle in front of it. Someone is mounting it; his feet are being strapped to the pedals by a young woman in white pants. The therapists hum around, checking people on the mats, going from patient to patient and circling around a big desk against the back wall. There's a wait. There is always a wait. I don't mind. I don't really feel the time passing, whether I'm waiting or not. I hear the clutter turning in my head that tells me of an unhappy future. I try to understand why I jumped in front of the train and the only answer I can come up with is that I couldn't take it anymore. Understanding what *it* is becomes the problem, turning in my head over and over again.

I look to the far end of the gym where the parallel bars are, bars that are so low that any able person could walk through them. Someone is going through them on an artificial leg, balancing and stepping forward carefully.

The middle of the room is covered with mats and that is where I do my exercises to strengthen my thighs. The mats are filled and the back wall is lined with patients in wheelchairs who are waiting to get on them. Next to me is a man who is paralyzed. His physical therapist is having him do exercises to move his head, working with a hand mirror so he can watch himself. He's smiling and making jokes about something that happened in his room last night and the therapist is bantering with him and laughing.

On the other side of me is an amputee who is sitting in a wheelchair but is handcuffed to it and a policeman stands alongside him and they're talking and I keep hearing the word Riker's. They're smiling too. All of this filters in as I look back at the cars going along the FDR and the sun bouncing off the river.

One of the therapists interrupts my ruminating by asking me to come over to a newly empty mat. She looks at my wheelchair and asks if I wheel in circles. I say sometimes. She says that she'll get me a special wheelchair as soon as she can that is operable with one hand. She asks me to dismount the wheelchair and lie on the mat. I do. Then she puts a leg weight on my left leg and tells me to do raises, three reps of ten. She asks me if I ever smile, she smiles, and then she leaves and goes to the next mat where a woman is doing the same exercise. I begin to do my repetitions. I look at the ceiling. It is high from where I am. It seems like a vaulted auditorium ceiling.

I'm lying in bed again. The sun coming through the window. Now I know the floor better. I know the patient who first brought me into the dayroom. The man who leans only leans when he gets his methadone. When he is not nodding on it, he waits for it by the nurses' station, but he likes me and tells me about his days of chasing the bag and nodding out with his girlfriend who OD'd. The woman on the floor exposes herself sometimes and the nurses ask her to cover herself and sometimes she responds but mostly she lies on the floor staring at the end of the hallway as if it were the exit which it is not. The man in the wheelchair never talks. He just mumbles and kicks out of time with the music coming from the speaker in the hall.

A nurse comes in holding a coat that I've never seen before. She says that I'm to wear it because I'm going out in a van Uptown to get a fit for my leg. A student from the physical therapy floor, a short, bearded man with glasses, is assigned to chaperone me to the pros- thetist. This is the first time I've been outside of the hospital since being under the train. I don't know what the hospital looks like outside the floor. It is big, people going back and forth around me, people sitting in chairs waiting, so many people, so much space. Legs keep passing by the wheelchair and I can see the outside through the windows. When we hit the outside, it's like entering a new and uncharted world. The air is cold. I had forgot what it's like to be cold. The only semblance I'd had of it was the redness in the cheeks of my father and mother and the other visitors. Ten degrees, a wind chill factor of below zero; the things they discussed to fill time meant nothing to me.

Now I am out in it. Hustled into a van, up a ramp, and taken up the same highway I watch from the window of the physical therapy room. Speed is strange. I haven't felt speed or looked out the passenger window of a car in a long time.

The prosthetist is all the way Uptown on a busy street. This is a street. A street, and I am on it and people are passing, so many people. They unload me, taking the chains off the wheelchair that held me braced in the van, get me over the curb and into the building. There are rails on the wall and a row of tiny rooms. I am put into one room and asked to wait. I sit with the student for a long time, feeling dull in my head, saying nothing. He tries to make conversation but it falls flat on me. I can't participate. Finally a man comes in who apologizes for the wait and begins to take measurements of my leg and make a cast of the stump. He smiles at me and says something about me wanting it to be right and that I don't want to walk cockeyed. He smiles and I nod and he asks me if I ever smile.

Lying down in my room. The loops seem to have run their course. No matter what I was doing, I was always preoccupied. The loops kept me busy. They kept me dull and dreary. I had investigated every perspective and every possibility ten times. I jump in front of a train. I want to be dead. I'm not. Things don't look bright. In fact they make me want to die more. But I am bored now, bored with these contemplations and in these contemplations there is even a line of thought that wants to know how to make this livable and how to go on. Now I am bored with even that. The hospital is boring. There is time and more time and nothing to fill it with except smoking and chatting with the patients who smoke and chat. The conversations are banal.

I have to do something if I'm not going to think all the time. Then it becomes apparent that even if I don't plan on coming out of all this alive I have to fill my time while I wait. The notebook is there. I begin with the alphabet, making letters with my left hand that look like they've been written by a frightened half-literate, scribbles, shaky lines. The alphabet becomes boring and so I start a small journal whose entries are sentences that take long minutes to write out. "I hate it here . . ."

## SUMMER 1988

I lay the chariot card from the tarot deck down on the table, it is a declaration of war. I leave a message on my psychiatrist's answering machine and put on the Sex Pistols blaring, waiting for it all to happen.

It is eight in the morning and I haven't slept all night even after I drank a whole bottle of Benadryl trying to knock myself out and there was only tingling and then numbness in my extremities. It isn't until seven in the morning that I realize I should try the Navane instead, that it isn't only insomnia.

Then I think it is a false alarm, an isolated incident. This happens sometimes. I get back on the Navane and I feel OK. Is it my anniversary? If it is, it's about six months early. It starts to creep up on me again. Anxiety. Restlessness. Agitation. I start taking my Klonopin and Navane every four hours. Sitting in my apartment I feel like I am going to climb the walls. I know I need more Navane. I put a call through to my doctor and at first I think I'll go downstairs and threaten the counselor with violence like I was a bomb ready to explode and she'll call the cops and the ambulance and they'll come and get me, first on line for Navane in the emergency room, but that kind of behavior will get me handcuffs and I don't want to be labeled or treated as violent so then I think I'll go down to the emergency room and wait there to be taken care of but that will be all night, and so I think I'll sit it out all night, turn on music and the TV loud to drown it out. In the morning I'll get my new prescription of Klonopin to the pharmacist and take it.

I admit myself to Gracie Square Hospital without an escort. I am going through this with my head on straight. When I get up to the psych ward I put my things away and get a cup of decaf coffee and sit down in the room where everyone eats. I'm not disoriented and I know how this goes pretty much so I ask where the patient in charge of welcoming patients is. They don't seem to have one. After checking out the ward I realize there is nothing to do, I don't know anyone and so I can't make conversation, and conversation and smoking pass the time, but with just smoking you pass the time until you're out of cigarettes but conversation gets you into a clique and a clique has people who have cigarettes and who'll give you cigarettes if you're in the clique. I look around for attractive women, being bored, and feeling sort of horny. I don't think I really want to try to make it with anyone but it would pass the time. Sitting at a table like solidified brilliant light is the most beautiful woman I've ever been in a room with. She gets up and comes over to me. She walks stiffly and her eyes are unnaturally alive. She stands so close that our noses are almost touching and she asks if I have a best man. I say yes, right away. She asks his name. I say the first name that pops into my head. She asks where we will live. I say Downtown. She asks if I mean at first. I say yes. She asks where we will live later. I say in a house. She asks where. I say in France. She asks how many rooms. I say six. She asks the color of the walls. I say beige. She asks what kind of heating system we will have. I say we will have a fireplace and gas heat. She asks what the first child's name will be. I say the first name that pops into my head, and she frowns and walks away.

I'm standing there knowing my child is wrongly named, knowing I've lost my wife, and I don't go after her, I just stand there. Then I turn to follow and she's gone. I go into the TV room looking for her and she's not there. I look around the room. I want to ask one of the patients if they've seen her, but I can't say her name. I know that I must have been born with it written inside me but I can't bring it up. I sit down on the couch chastising myself for losing her when the guy sitting next to me sticks his nicotine-fingered hand over my lap and tells me his name. I shake the hand. He talks and goes on and on and I'm only half listening because I'm trying to bring up that name. The talking wears me down and then I'm listening, listening to him talk about Jerome, and I don't know who Jerome is, and so have to make inferences along the way until I receive the whole thing.

Jerome is here. He is in the hospital and he stole ten dollars from Gene and Gene wants it back, but he can't go into Jerome's room to get it back because he's mad about territories. He says that he has to live with the fact that he is not allowed to walk certain places or move in certain directions and he knows it's mad. He once drove a hundred miles out of his way just to get from Manhattan to New Jersey, but it's the way it is and no medication is going to convince him that it isn't that way.

Because I'm his sergeant since I shook his hand, Gene wants me to go into Jerome's room and he'll give me five of the ten when I find it. I'm not interested in money but I need help in the search for the woman so I tell him about her and he agrees to scour the floor look-ing for her as soon as he gets his ten dollars.

We go to Jerome's room and no one is in there. Gene says that it's probably tucked in a belonging or under something. I ask him how he knows that Jerome doesn't have it on him, and Gene says that he knows because Jerome always goes back to his room before using the snack machine and comes out with money. He says he'll stand watch while I go in and if a nurse is coming he'll say there's a fire in the hole, and then I get my ass out.

I feel nervous but I don't know why because I am God or a god or godlike, being Christ, and Christ threw the money changers out of the temple so I am justified in Scriptures in my deed of justice. I go into the room ready to ransack it with speed but when I get in, there are no belongings. Nothing. I go under the pillow and there's just some change and I look under the bed, crouching as far as the artificial leg can take me, and there's just some dust bunnies. Then Gene calls into the room and I come quickly out. I report to him. He is dissatisfied. He refuses to go on my search with me for my wife and walks away.

I am angry and I have to go to the bathroom, so I go there and I stand next to this skinny guy at the urinals. His shirt has his name on it and a credo—Jerome Takes No Shit. I feel brave because I am immortal and invin-cible and ask Jerome where the ten dollars is. He asks me what ten dollars. I tell him that I am talking about the ten dollars that he stole from Gene. He wants to know who Gene is. So I describe Gene. Jerome says that he didn't take anybody's ten dollars and Gene is a lying motherfucker. He says that all whites are lying motherfuckers except the off-whites and then he asks me if I am a white or an off-white. I am Christ and I don't lie, therefore I'm off-white by his definition and I tell him I am. He says that if I am off-white, I will go tell Gene he is a lying motherfucker. He washes his hands and leaves.

Now I am really filled with the power of justice and retribution as I walk into the TV room to find Gene slouched on the couch with a cigarette watching TV. I walk up to him, right in front of him, and call him a lying motherfucker.

He tells me to sit down next to him. He says I must have walked into Jerome's polluted territory to get an idea like that, and he says we'll go into Jerome's room again to find the ten dollars. Then it is lunchtime and I know I'll get to see the woman and hear her name called out for her tray, but she isn't there. Gene says that she must be eating in her room, or in restraints, or in seclusion. What if she is in seclusion? Then I'll never find her. The thought is like a black crow over me.

After lunch I sit with Gene in the TV room waiting for when the time is right to go out on another run of justice. Gene is good at diagnosing all the patients sitting in the room. When he gets to me, he says I am Christ. I ask him how he knows and he says it is apparent. From that moment on I know I am white and whites are no lying motherfuckers and Jerome must have stolen ten dollars if Gene says he did. This is just reality.

Gene says that what I ought to do if I am really serious about finding this girl is to make a room check like the nurses do. I think this is a great idea and so I go from room to room peeking in, careful not to let the nurses see what I am up to. At the end of my check there are three beds that have patients in them, and one could be her. They are all wrapped up in covers.

I go into the dayroom and sit by the clock and every five minutes I go back to those rooms. It becomes my activity. Then after two hours have passed and my faith begins to wane, she is there sitting up in bed with a drowsy look on her face. I look at her and she looks at me for an eternal moment and it all seems unreal. Then without saying anything she goes into the bathroom and the door closes behind her. She has disappeared again and I have something to say to her although I'm not certain what and I go into the bathroom after her.

So close to her now, the bathroom tiles seem to hum. She is sitting on the toilet and I look away to give her privacy and find myself looking into the bathroom mirror. The moment is so loud in my ears that I don't hear the sound of my fly zip down. I don't feel anything below my neck and I can feel my face only because I can see it in the mirror and it is red and looks like I am bench-pressing. Then I feel my hip lurch against the sink and hug the sink trying to brace my prosthetic leg which feels as though it is about to give way. SIN. This is Sin. And I'm numb. I'm numb to sin.

It is over when my mouth opens in the mirror and my disembodied legs come back and my fly is zipped up, and I sneak out like a thief hoping not to see a nurse.

I see her later. She passes by the open door of the TV room and goes into the dayroom and sits down. I point her out to Gene. He tells me that if we got off to a bad start then I shouldn't go up to her empty-handed. I should bring her a present. An engagement gift.

The ideas spin in my head. What is available to me? I have clothes. I have books. None of these things seems right. I go into the kitchen. There are plastic forks, and spoons and napkins and sugar packets and stirrers but

nothing appeals to me. It has to be something as beautiful as she is, and then it strikes me. The stove, the
burners, fire. I can handle it. I can bring her fire. I pile
the napkins high on one of the burners and turn on the
gas. It goes up slower than I thought it would and then
the water starts coming down from the ceiling, and they
put me in seclusion.

If I go through that doorway I'll pass escape velocity.
I'll never come down then. I must remember that. The
mad are out there. That's why they put me here with a
woman blocking the door, to protect me. I know what I
am. I've seen Mary Magdalene. That's her name. They've
taken everything out of this room so I can think. They
want me to think hard. My vision is fuzzy so I won't be
distracted. The woman is a blur outside, just a mass
of color and after I finish thinking about her colors I
will be free. White. Brown. White. Brown. White. Brown.
White. Me. Christ. Put a sign upon my forehead. They've
removed my leg so I have to stay here and think hard
about the one thing that is in this room: the bedpan. It
must be special. It must stand for something or do more
than to be pissed and shit in. Bedpan. Pan. Frying.
Eggs. Womb. Woman. Man. Me. Christ. Put a sign upon
my forehead. My father is Joseph, he drinks and is
nostalgic. My mother is Mary, she is protective and likes
to cook. My brother is James, he works as a clerk. I can
feel Mary Magdalene warm inside me just as I feel the
whole world warm inside me like food. I rock with it,
nurture it, amazed how its immensity can be shrunk.
Everything, every country, all the people in them, all
their joys and tragedies wiped away within me. It happens effortlessly, it's natural, it's what I'm promised
to be. I rock and rock so satisfied and so peaceful that
I see the woman outside the door smiling. She must

be smiling. Everything is so quiet. I can see a figure beyond her outside in the madness. Is it Mary M., Mary C., Joseph or James? Have they come for me? I'm not finished yet. I'm not finished scouring the world. I feel Satan in my stomach and work him through with good thoughts of myself. He fights like an unruly child but he gives in and is absorbed in me. Now I can feel it all peeling away, the material identity, the last pieces, I discard my name. I discard my past. I discard Canarsie. I discard Manhattan. I discard the football league. I discard JFK Airport. I discard them all into Mary M. She can eat their names like I'm eating the rest: Staten Island. Nova Scotia. Indonesia . . . and even the words I speak, I discard the English language. I discard all emotions except for love and happiness. I live in peace. It's like I'm floating on a life raft in the middle of the ocean and that's where I want to be. In the barren ocean. In the barren desert. The temptations are coming to me in the form of little pills and I refuse them. They come three times a day. Then they give me the needle and I merge with sleep. It's like I collide in midair with sleep and the difference between being asleep and being awake is minimal. I still think. I'm still aware. I see shapes: squares, diamonds, circles, triangles, and they're all dancing and making up a new place to be. I see animals and they don't frighten me. I see demons and I turn them back into squares and diamonds. I see faces and they have no names and they turn into shapes. Then the shapes turn into lines and I follow the lines while I sleep until I reach the end of the line which is the beginning of a new shape and I choose to wake up.

There is a man outside the door now. He's fuzzy but I can see by his angles that he is a man, and he is brown

and white and brown and white and he talks to me. He
asks me how I'm doing and I say fine after I rediscover
the language to answer him. He says that I'm awfully
quiet. I say nothing because this doesn't sound like a
question. Then I say I'm using the bedpan. I look at the
bedpan. Frying pan. Eggs. Breasts. Woman. Man. Me.
Christ. Put a sign upon my forehead. It always comes
out the same. I try again. Bedpan. Bed. Sleep. Good.
Me. Christ. Put a sign upon my forehead. Bedpan. Bed.
Lovers. Woman. Man. Me. Christ. Put a sign upon my
forehead. Bedpan. Bed. Pillow. Soft. Woman. Man. Me.
Christ. Put a sign upon my forehead. The doorway.
When I'm finished thinking and changing I'll go through
the doorway and the madness will be gone. The man at
the doorway is calling to the nurses' station, he's asking
if he can be relieved for a moment, and I know that if
the door is unprotected, even for a moment, the madness will get in. I say no, but he doesn't listen to me
and he gets up and goes off. Now the madness rushes in
and I know I am mad. I am infected. I am ill. There is no
safe place to be except within myself and I start by iden-
tifying myself—I am Christ but it comes up I am not
Christ. I run inside myself looking for Christ in me and
come up empty. I'm scared. What am I? I'm no thing
now. Afraid, I loiter in the vacancy. No name. No past.
No mother. No father. No brother. No life. This is suicide
catching up to me. This is spontaneous suicide. This is
living suicide. I'm afraid. Then I look into the vacancy
and the answer comes back to me: if I am to be Christ I
must suffer. When everything is gone, hold on to the
pain. Only the pain is left. But the vacancy is not finished, it is going to tell me truths I do not want to know.
This is rigged. This is monitored. This is conducted.
This has been orchestrated. Ever since you were born.

This is an experiment. This is a Christ-maker experiment. THE PAST IS A LIE. THEY'VE SURGICALLY RE-MOVED YOUR LEG. THEY'VE REMOVED YOUR ARM. THEY'VE ALTERED YOUR SIGHT. I scream without stopping.

## SUMMER 1989

I get on the bus to go to my volunteer job and feel I have to get off so I get off at the next stop, then I feel I should go so I wait for the bus, and when it comes I stand in front of the doors and watch them close. Then I feel I should go so I wait for the bus, and I get on and go two stops and get off, and I walk up the block to the next avenue so I can take that bus home, and I wait for the bus, and then I feel I should go so I walk back just in time to catch the bus. Now I am all out of tokens so I walk home and smoke.

I smoke. I think. I smoke.

The waiting area at the clinic has a sign that says NO SMOKING, but the people there smoke anyway. I sit in a plastic seat waiting for my appointment. There's a man looking at the magazines. He sits back down and then gets up and looks at the magazines again never taking one. A woman smokes at the back of the room. I go into the bathroom and have a cigarette in an effort to half obey the wishes of the clinic. In the bathroom the sink and the urinals and the toilets are crowded with butts and the air is filmy with smoked cigarettes.

I come back out and the woman is gone but the man is still there and he goes back to the magazine rack and studies the magazines and sits down. I'm blocking at the wall, trying to zero out, waiting for it to break. I'm pounding at the wall with my eyes trying to put it between me and the tension. If I can concentrate very hard I can numb it away. I stare. I wait. I stare. The tension goes up and down all day.

Then while I'm staring at the same spot I've been staring at for the last ten minutes, it breaks. I feel it. It's as if my shoulders have raised up into my head and now they ease back into position. Everything is all right now. The world and I are on good terms and everything is peaceful.

I meet my doctor in a cubicle for a short session. My mood is good now and I have nothing to say, but when I'm in the street it drops again like a rock and I walk home lost from everything. I walk up my block to Columbus Avenue and stop at the corner wanting to go back to the house. I walk back down the block halfway and then I turn back and head up the block again. The same thing happens at the streetlight at Columbus and 106th. I stop. I turn back walking the length of the block and then I stop again and head back toward the clinic.

Now I walk home from the clinic taking Amsterdam Avenue and everything is mixed up inside me. The street is full of people and I envy them for knowing where they are going. I want to go back to the clinic but I don't. What can they do? I want to go back home but I don't want to go back. How can it help? Outside the Hungarian Pastry Shop people are sitting enjoying the view of the cathedral and drinking coffee. Outside the Peace Fountain people are sunning themselves and looking at the sculpture. A peacock is all the way in the back and is no hallucination. They keep peacocks on the grounds behind the fountain. The sun is coming down strong and the women have sunglasses and skirts on. Their strides are full of purpose. I want to stride with them. I keep walking, trying not to stop, trying to go forward, and to keep going forward for the few blocks it takes me to get back home but at Amsterdam and 106th I stop. I feel myself hovering, directionless. It takes a lot of will to pull me back on track and get me going down 106th Street, but I do and I reach the corner and soon I am home.

I sit in my room. Monitoring my moods. They keep changing and as they dip I want to run. When the blocking becomes useless and the tension mounts there's no place to go but out. There's really no place to go, so I sit some more, smoking, staring. I stare. I wait. I stare. Then the mood dips another degree and I'm feeling choked and have to get out. I'm going to the park which is only a block away but it's a long indecisive block. I stop at the corner ready to go back to the apartment and then I bring myself to push forward to Central Park West. I cross the street, sit down on a bench, and begin to feel better watching the cars pass. I look up at the old dilapidated nursing home that looks like a mansion. It's out of place and time, like the peacocks at the Peace Fountain, and I don't know how or why but it gets me over. I begin to feel better and a person walks by and I smile at him. I feel the relief as if a horrible and sharp spasm has been massaged out. I go to Central Park at 103rd Street and sit by the pond. This is more scenic. The sun comes down on the water and the birds chirp and bicyclers go over the small bridge, but I sink again. I block, staring at a duck on the pond and then shifting my gaze to the bicycle path. I light up a cigarette. It gives no relief. I get no relief from the scenery. It all feels the same as my room. It all feels hard and remote.

I want to go back to my room. I walk halfway up the path and then stop. Then I start again reaching the street and then I stop and turn back. I turn again and head back to the house. I go back to my room and sit with the radio and television off while I try to think my way out somehow. Is there some activity? Something I could do that would give some relief? There's only sleep. With sleep I have a chance of waking up in a lighter mood. I lie down and try to relax myself. Slowly. Slowly. It's like closing my eyes and grabbing onto something fast and hard to catch. First I watch under my eyelids and then I wait for that non sequitur thought that tells me that I'm being pulled into unconsciousness. I see the image of an eagle and then I'm asleep.

The morning mood is light blue. I'm rehashing my dream, it's a crush from junior high again, in my old bedroom in my mother's house. My crush keeps saying that she loves me while a fat raccoon, a fugitive from summer camp, nibbles at my feet. This is definitely light blue . . .

I wake up like that, slip into a pair of sweatpants, a sock, and a T-shirt and go down to the Park West House dining room in my wheelchair because I feel breakdown. Whether I compensate for swelling or shrinking by adjusting stump socks, I am still getting breakdown on the stump that puts me in the wheelchair.

It's ten o'clock. All the residents have already left for the program. In the morning I like being alone with my coffee, with the coffee urn, with my keys, my lighter and my cigarettes. The dining room television is off. I'm remembering my dream and playing a song in my head. I think that will be enough protection against my thoughts, but they wake up and push their way through the dream and the song and everything's shot to hell.

I look into the ashtray and see five snubbed-out cigarettes that I smoked while retracing my dream and I
throw up a picture of the Grim Reaper with a handful
of chemotherapy pills. The horror makes me have to
smoke another cigarette. Then the image subsides and I
see that my thoughts will be operating like a wolf pack:
attack and pull back.

Today I go to the support group. Coming upstairs
from the dining room and into my apartment I don't
want to go to my group—I want to sit and smoke until
four o'clock when I go downstairs and join the residents
for a cup of coffee and sit and smoke some more. I make
a truce, a compromise. A van comes to pick me up and
take me to the support group. When it comes I'll decide.

Sitting in my apartment I feel myself slipping. The
mood changes. It floats in a dull blue-gray. I feel inert. I
don't want to go anywhere.

The telephone rings. It's the downstairs office telling
me the van is outside. I don't want to go but I see my
day before me if I don't. Thinking. Smoking. Thinking.
Feeling the mood dip lower and lower and fighting it
back like floodgates. I'm going. I'm going because I want
to ride in the van. I'm going for the ride. I roll downstairs
and the driver meets me at the curb. I know him, but we
don't say hello. He loads me into the back of the ambulette and secures the wheelchair with a chain. We hit
the West Side Highway with a view of the river and I
think this mood is yellow like the sun flaring on the
cars. The speed and air go through my head lifting me.
Cars are going by and falling back and I watch them,
feeling better. Then the ambulette begins to slow and
merge with traffic. We get stuck in traffic which mutes
my yellow mood. Stationed in traffic, thinking about my
handicap, I take a dip. I say to myself that I shouldn't

be so soft, so self-pitying. There are a lot of people who are handicapped, some much worse than I am, but it doesn't work. The feelings have their own volition. They have teeth. I feel boxed in the back of the van, my wheelchair chained to the floor, caught between my feelings. I can feel myself sinking. I know it's good I'm chained to the floor of a vehicle in traffic instead of being in the vicinity of a sharp instrument. It's a dangerous feeling. It's the same feeling I felt on the subway platform. It's making the pact. A car beeps its horn and brings me back to where I am until the light changes and the traffic clears up a little. Some air comes through the front windows relieving me and the river is sparkling with afternoon light. The cars begin to separate. I feel it all lifting and leveling off.

The group is a blur. I fall away, feeling mute and out of touch, listening and not hearing, and when I'm asked to speak I can only say that I have nothing to say. When I get back in the van I feel better knowing I'll be going for the ride and the ride fulfills its promise. There is no traffic and the ambulette speeds down the West Side Highway keeping me level for the length of the ride.

When I get to the residence I go downstairs to the dining room where a few residents are waiting for dinner. The television plays on, no one is watching it. It just fills up the room. I feel myself sinking again coming off the ride and falling back into a flat space. I stare at the wall in the dining room trying to determine if I should go upstairs or not, which is better? I light up a cigarette to give me time to decide. Everything is dead. It's dead when it stops to think. Keep moving. Go upstairs. What's upstairs? There's more of you upstairs. Fewer things to put between you and . . . I'm already in the elevator going upstairs, through the hall, to my apartment.

Inside the mood is deeply dark. Black.

It's almost dinnertime and everybody must be lining up at the kitchen. I can't go. I lie down. I'm in a down-spin lying on my bed. Going down and down until I hear myself think that I'd rather be dead. I wallow in it. I feel its pull on me like a hole. I'm in, and I know it will pass so I have to weather it out.

I wake up the next morning and it doesn't wait. I don't even remember sleeping. It hits immediately and with an evil familiarity. I go down to the dining room and I smoke but the cigarettes don't taste good. I can feel the tension in my head behind my eyes. I'm thinking I'm going to have to try to force out some grandiosity. Even if I can't make myself believe I'm God at least I have to . . . but no, I need to be God.

There's no power of suggestion that can take me there. I go back to my room and the apartment feels like it's closing in on me. My things are my enemies, the lamp, the wall, the window, nothing will stand between me and the pressure. I want to go out but my leg is bad so I ice it with an ice cube and a paper towel hoping that I can bring the swelling down so I can go to the park. It's raining. I don't care.

Rubbing the inside of my leg with the ice, I can hear the rain coming down. It's a heavy rain with thunder and inexplicably my mood begins to break. I feel waves of relaxation through my head. I've found a place to hide.

I turn on the radio. I turn on the television. I want as much company as I can fill the room with and even with all this, the rain, the thunder, the television, the radio, I begin to sink again.

I rub furiously with the ice hoping to numb the area enough to get into the leg. I put it on and I don't feel the pain. I get dressed with a coat and hood and go outside. The rain is coming down so hard that the streets are empty. A wet cat hides under a parked car seemingly bewildered by the force of the downpour. I start to walk and I begin to feel the spot on my stump. First it's a tingle, then a throb, and then at reaching Central Park West it's a shooting pain.

Now I can go back to the house and face the apartment or I can go on. I take a step back, then a step forward. A bus passes and I imagine the people inside are watching me dance on the corner in a growing puddle. Go to the park. I go. I go to the duck pond limping, in the pouring rain trying to run from my head. Every step is like a knife stuck up into the middle of my stump.

Soaking, I sit down on the bench and look at the pond. Not a thing is reflected in it. The rain is pelting it. Up on the bike path I can see a few stubborn joggers making it through the rain. My leg hurts. I want a cigarette.

I take out the pack and manage to light one in the rain. I'm soaked through to the skin and my sneakers seem like sponges. I stare at the drops coming down from the willow tree that dips into the pond. It leans under the weight of the rain. The ducks aren't out. Thunder booms in the distance. I drag from my cigarette and it doesn't help much. The leg aches. In order to get back through the few blocks it takes to get home I'm going to have to feel that knife going up my stump at every step, but even that isn't as bad as my fear that my mood will get blacker and I'll keep falling and falling until I have to think about killing myself. Making the pact is the worst part or just before making the pact, when there is still hope. After the pact is made it's only a matter of accomplishing the task. It's only a matter of getting up enough nerve and energy. I've been running. Running from the pact. I've been tumbling from black to blue and I can't do this anymore. This is insane. I can't run anymore, I just have to sit with it and hope that it has a bottom.

# SUMMER 1990

In the white room I can't sleep. The insides of my eyelids are unsafe. In the white room when I open my eyes the wall comes alive like mad static on a black and white television. Boxes. I see radiant boxes when I close my eyes. They are not coming at me, they go in a line away from me but they glow as brightly as the headlights of an oncoming car. They are in a line heading for a point of perspective, with boxes on top and boxes on bottom as if I were flying in a helicopter moving fast over a huge warehouse of glowing boxes.

When I open my eyes to get away from them the wall begins to come alive with dots, a cloud of dots that turns into a shape as if a television were clearing to show its picture. I know the shape. I've seen it everywhere. It's the eye. It looks like that strange eye on the dollar bill with its big pupil. It's the eye, and I am all right with the eye but going down the wall the eye changes into a flutter of angels, the kind that are cut from paper, no definition but definitely angels, and I'm OK with the angels. They are good. But further down the wall the space between the fluttering angels turns into diamond shapes and those shapes turn into spiders, and I'm almost OK with the spiders, it's the next thing, the horned demon shapes or angry ghosts that scare the hell out of me and when they come off the wall and I can no longer turn them back like I've been doing all night, I close my eyes and go back to the bright boxes.

In the white room with a high rectangular window with black curtains, I know I'm where I'm supposed to be because the song says so and if the song says it then it's where I should be.

Someone must have slipped me acid.

Someone must have slipped me a lot of acid. I must have the acid content of a generation in me. It must have come through the songs I listen to. I am the Messiah the children of the sixties were waiting for and I've got their blood in me and I know it's my fuel but it's also my poison.

The boxes become too bright and I have to open my eyes to the wall again. Eye. Angels. Spiders. Demons. And then I close my eyes to make them stop.

Then I look at the boxes again. They move faster and faster. Brighter and brighter and I open my eyes. The wall fills with dots. Eye. Angels. Spiders. Demons.

I can't do this anymore. I can't. I've got to make it stop, but I can't. This must be another test, or I'm out of control, and I must be stopped.

I close my eyes. Boxes. Bright boxes searing the insides of my eyelids. I open my eyes. Eye. Angels. Spiders. Demons.

I have to take it. I have to ride it like I've been riding it all night, but what if something is wrong, what if I am out of control?

I wheel out to the ER nurses' station and tell the nurse that I must be stopped and she tells me to go back to my room.

The wall comes alive again with its cloud of static. Eye. Angels. Spiders. Demons. I close my eyes. Boxes.

Unbelievably bright boxes. They hurt. They sear. I wheel back out to the nurses' station and the words come to me. I say that I'm seeing hypnagogic visions and something has to be done and she medicates me with yellow liquid from a small cup and puts me in the dark middle room alone to let me sleep.

"So we caught the Zodiac Killer," says the ER security man outside the door and I know he means me, and that everything that I am thinking, that I am God, and what I see, and what I've come to believe, is a huge psychotic smoke screen that blocks what I have done. It clouds the fact that I killed all those women in the newspaper. I panic. A man comes in and gives me a questionnaire while I try to ask him questions that will eliminate me as the murderer. I try to form a question that will let me know what I have done, and who I am, but at the same time not directly enough to implicate me. Now if he begins to ask me questions about dates and women, I'll know he is after me. He puts his clipboard in front of me and giving me his pen asks me to draw a circle. I laugh, relieved.

He asks me some questions and he leaves. Now I am alone in the dark middle room waiting for what will come out of the darkness. I still see the boxes under my eyelids but the eye and the angels and the spiders and the demons after them don't show in this room. I begin to feel myself go into a relaxed state, not sleep, but relaxed, tired, but sleep won't come.

It's like this for a while, staring into the darkness, feeling my body going down the bed. Then I hear a familiar voice outside the door of the room and the door opens. It's one of my counselors from the residence. He says that they're not holding me and he's come to take me home.

It's morning. The ER waiting area that was crowded and noisy last night is now empty and almost quiet. We go out on Amsterdam Avenue and catch a cab and I feel I'm released now to fulfill my destiny as the air comes in the window and brings me out of the relaxed state I found in the middle room.

When we get to my apartment and my counselor lets me in I find that the whole apartment has been cleaned. The books have been tidied and put back against the wall in stacks three rows deep.

I haven't slept in twenty-four hours, but I feel energized. I feel like going for a walk. I need to walk. I leave the house making a right and heading down the street to Manhattan Avenue and then go to Central Park West and before I know it I'm at 103rd Street at the duck pond. I walk over to a tree and sit under it. Now I'm sitting under the tree and looking at the grass and I want to watch it grow so I flatten out in the grass, and I begin to roll back and forth in it like a dog. I'm a dog. I've got no cares in the world and I'm rolling in the grass.

A woman passes by and gives me a strange look but I don't care, I keep rolling for a while and then I head back to the house. I look at my watch and it lies to me. There is no place to be, no reason to tell time. THERE ARE NO CLOCKS IN THE KINGDOM OF HEAVEN.

On Manhattan Avenue I pass a garbage pail, and an idea that is almost a vision comes to me. The beginning of the New Age with no time and no possessions starts here with me. I will go to my bank account and withdraw all my money in singles and fill this garbage can and take it to Rockefeller Center and give out singles on the street. That will be the beginning.

I go to my apartment looking for my bankcard. It is always in my wallet and my wallet is always in the pocket of my jeans but the wallet isn't there. Where is my wallet? There is money on the kitchen table, bills and change, but no wallet. Did I put it away before I went to the ER? I look in the night table drawer in my bedroom pulling out everything and soon I'm standing in papers with addresses and phone numbers from a long time ago, ATM receipts, condoms, appliance manuals, warrantees, comic books, envelopes, photographs, stump socks, gift wrapping paper, looseleaf paper, old mail, paper clips, and magazines. It's all over the floor. I step through it going to the next possible spot: the clothes drawer. I pull out socks, underwear, shirts, pants, until it's all over the floor. No wallet.

Maybe when they cleaned up . . . they could have put it anywhere. My eyes fall on the closet. Inside there are stacks of art supplies: pads, canvases, illustration boards, and a paint box. I pull them all out and now with the paint box next to the clothes I realize what I must do, why I was brought to the bedroom.

I take out the paints, about to paint the name of God on all of my shirts. But it must not be *God*. How do I signify the name of God without writing *God?* I go into the living room looking for the Bible in the stacks of books against the wall and soon I'm standing in a sea of hardcover and paperback books. I can't find the Bible but I do find a mythology book and without looking through it I know what god I'll be on my shirt.

Today is Wednesday. Woden's day. I am Woden.

I go back into the bedroom and taking out brush and paint begin to paint a shirt with a big *W* and a dot on top of it for power. I drape it over a chair to dry.

Now that I've accomplished this I am ready to sleep. I lie down but I can't stay down. I can't sit. I can't stand. I pace. I pace in the hallway between the living room and the bedroom. I go back to the bedroom. I lie down. I can't stay down. I pace. I'm tense. I'm on fire. I strip and take a shower. I lie down in bed. I can't stay down. I have to get dressed and go up to Emily's apartment.

Get dressed. The room is full of things. I can't distinguish between a condom and a sock. It takes a long time before I can distinguish what are my clothes and then I don't know in what order to put them on. Everything is made up of colors. Think of the order of the rainbow. Red. Orange. Yellow. Green. Blue. Indigo. Violet. The red things come first. My sneakers are white and my jeans are blue. White must come before blue and I put on my sneakers first and then have to squeeze my jeans over them.

Up to Emily's apartment. Emily's not home. I run back down to my apartment and take a wad of bills off of the table and head outside to Columbus Avenue. It's evening now. Standing outside of the sandwich shop is a woman. I know her. I've seen her before. She's the only way I'm getting to sleep and I need to sleep very very badly.

I bring her into the apartment, into the bedroom, already having paid her on the street and we strip down. I'm interested in having an orgasm as fast as I can. I do and she leaves. Now I lie down in bed. I get up. I pace. I lie down. I get up. I pace.

I turn on the television. I watch the porn on public access in my apartment because I'm wired with carnality. Even after several ejaculations it doesn't stop, the women don't become boring and the plots don't become ridiculous. When I've expelled it physically my mind is still with it and the graphic nudity almost becomes literal. The women become graphic, even more they become like reading a book, their visuals become a story.

I'm not just looking at it, I'm reading it. I'm not ogling it over a drink looking up from a tabletop or turning them into masturbatory figures in a magazine. The strippers aren't titillating after a point, they're something else. I'm feeding them into my head like they're the Dow Jones.

It's time to visit Harold because I know Harold is up now. I knock on his door. I can see the window to his bedroom from the hall. The shade is down. I call across the empty center shaft of the building to ask if he's in bed. Nothing. Wait. Then the door opens. He asks why I said that. I say what. He says that I said I want him dead. I say I didn't say that. He insists that I did. I insist I asked him if he was in bed. He lets me in, but he's still upset. His hands are shaking very badly. I cure it by telling him to straighten and bend his hands. We have tea. We stay up all night listening to classical music.

We stay up until dawn having great philosophical discussions about associative semantics and then he goes to bed. I go to my apartment to wait for the urge to sleep. I baby-sit myself with MTV. Videos that I normally criticize for the music, or the banality of the video, are totally engaging now because the visuals are the story. Colors, faces, clothes, women, one twenty-four-hour montage that reads like a fast-moving picture book of colors, faces, clothes, and women.

I lie down again with the TV still on in the living room feeling that now I can meet sleep in midair. I relax. I keep myself on the bed. There is a brief and bright flash under my eyelids and then I spring up as if I had ten hours of sleep.

There is coffee and smoking and talk in the dining room and talk is like food, because alone with my own mind it begins to devour itself. It breaks up into anywhere from twelve to what I eventually manage to break

down into three tracks of thought that have an argu-
mentative dialogue with each other. I feel them all in
my head at the same time and so I can't put on my
clothes while I think about the weather. I either put
on my clothes or think about the weather. Usually I just
sit with my mouth agape or humming while my mind
races on.

I try to take my medication but I've lost my ability to
count and separate and I take what I can.

I'm dressed, using the red, orange, yellow, green,
blue, indigo and violet method and heading for the program. I'm wearing my God shirt and I feel as if I'm being
announced as I go down every street and as I cross at
every light.

I get to the program and go up to the lounge and I am
struck by this woman. I think about talking to her and
then I am talking to her. Her name is Sharon and she
says her biggest problem is making friends. I say I can
get her friends, I have a whole address book stuffed with
friends and so I promise her I can help.

We walk to Riverside Park and talk and soon she has
to leave and I feel crestfallen. I go back to the residence,
to my apartment, and pace. I want to sleep but I can't
with all this tension so I go up to Emily's apartment,
and she's home and I bring her downstairs and we have
sex.

Emily leaves but I'm still tense, I'm still rushing. I'm
still wired, and so I go to my address book rifling it for
names and find Randi, an acquaintance but a possibility and I call her and leave a message on her answering
machine that I'd like to marry her tomorrow, but that
still isn't enough. I go through the address book again
and come up with Mary, call her, and I begin to describe
her anatomy to her. She knows something's wrong and

she stays on while I get more and more obscene.

After the phone call is over I watch the videos and then the porn on public access which distracts me enough to realize that my apartment is a mess.

How do I clean it? Like balancing colors in a painting. I study the mess for a long time like a chessboard and then I move one book to the other side of the room. Now the composition is balanced.

I pace again. I feel the agitation rising. I have to sleep. Swallowing 50 mg of cherry liquid Benadryl doesn't allow me to lie in bed. I can't stay on the mattress and yet desperately need a pause from the constant barrage of thoughts and the physical agitation. I roll back and forth in my wheelchair, the equivalent of pacing, like I am running a race to catch up with sleep. I increase the dosage to 100 mgs and roll back and forth in the wheelchair waiting for it to take effect, but after forty-five minutes there is no change. I down the bottle. I become numb and can lie down feeling the numbness in my extremities but when it wears off, I have not slept.

Lying in the bed, I close my eyes and under them staring at me is my face, looking like an insane pirate, with one bloodshot red eye. I have begun to dream without falling asleep. There is no protecting myself from what my subconscious can throw at me. Anything, even the most innocuous things can be horrifying to me in this state. Conscious, my mind is in overdrive, falling over itself, racing, and my body going with it, and now since it has been days since I have slept, my nightmares are coming. The insides of my eyelids aren't safe. Nothing is safe. They come on their own. Now I can't get off the bed and my eyelids are heavy and the line is becoming thin enough that it's hard for me to say if my eyes are open or closed. I am awake. I am conscious and I am dreaming. Then the knowledge that I am dreaming leaves but I am still conscious. The figures start coming more like live theater than cinema. First they form out of shapes and lines, and then they become full figures, malformed animals, hideous heads, and what look like devils, all as if they are trapped in a glass box looking up at me. Then the protective glass is gone, and we are looking into each other's eyes. They are as real as the bed or chair in my room. As they are about to cross the boundary I pull open my eyes and call out. I have to go to the hospital. They have to give me the medication that will put me into REM sleep and save me.

Going to the hospital I'm impressed by the way things flying by the back window of the ambulance are registering in my head before I see them, trees, streetlights, people. I know them before I see them. Put me out. Put me out. The ER doctor speaks to me but I can only half hear her. They give me some liquid and then I am asleep.

I awake the next day with a directing hard-on. I assess my situation. I go home.

Mary is a good friend who I hit like an alarm box, calling her up, making a prolonged obscene phone call.

I am sleeping with my neighbor Emily because I can't get sex from Sharon.

I am paying for sex when Emily isn't available.

I am in love with Sharon.

A force of nature is pulling me through the street, to the program and back, keeping me up all night, disallowing me to be alone for long, disallowing me to stay in my apartment, putting me out on the street because I have to be moving, and then all that willing that feels like it is coming from outside me seems to focus into a person. It's as if it is allegiance gained by hypnosis.

She said she needs friends and she is suicidal. She is waiting for the OK, some sign or mental capitulation. I told her I'd get her friends and that I was the sign that she should not commit suicide. We spend every afternoon in Riverside Park going from bench to bench, having long conversations about mysticism that are like Chinese boxes opening and building into bigger Chinese boxes. I come to believe, narrowing my power, that I am her personal Messiah come to save her and then that I am her personal Messiah come to seduce her. Time separates into time spent with her and time without her, and in those times I think of going over to what I think is her street and ringing all the buzzers on the block. I do so without finding her, not knowing her last name.

She says she can heal me of the belief that I am both Christ and Satan. When I'm God I feel supremacy and when I'm Satan I feel supreme control. She meditates and prays constantly, lying in bed with the problem for long hours. I can't relax. I am with her on the park bench, endeavoring to prove to her that I am right for her, more than right, I am ordained for her and that is why I feel no sin in trying to dislodge her from her boyfriend.

Nothing can be let go of until it is resolved with both sides not hating each other, and so phone calls volley back and forth on the inflection of a word. I wait for the signs in the atmosphere, a change on the shadow on the wall, the TV blinking, a word overheard from the residence office downstairs, as the prelude to her calling back. In-person arguments last five and six hours with peaks and valleys, epics where both parties come to terms but not because it is best, when they should end with someone walking away and not coming back.

I am not allowed up to her apartment and she won't go to mine. We meet at the program lounge and go to the park where it's neutral and almost time-free, no clocks, only the sun, and even then we can extend it past dusk. After a while of building to where we've talked more than most people do in a year, I'm invited to her apartment. This is different. It's intimate. I expect something will happen soon. We smoke and an ash burns her and I wonder why she pulls back. It's only heat. I burn myself all the time and I don't even feel it. With my mouth and nostrils full of smoke, sitting legs apart, I feel like Satan. I feel like I'm guiding affairs. She writes stories, and she takes out her writing for me to read. I read it and she pulls out more.

Then we're in her bedroom because she wants to show me something and I know the distance she puts between us means it's not going to happen now, but soon.

She pulls back the shower curtain and there is a cage with two white birds in it standing up in the tub. She says that they make such a mess that she has to keep them there or the bedroom gets full of seed, gravel, shit, and feathers. She can't stand it when they rustle. She can't stand when they squawk. They ruin her thinking. They make it hard to sleep. I ask her why she doesn't get rid of them. She says that she can't get them down to the ASPCA. She hasn't been able to. She wants to kill them. I ask why she doesn't, and she replies it's against her religious beliefs.

I say I'll kill the birds for her. I might do it with a hammer and something to cover them, I don't know. I'm not thinking about how they'll suffer if I kill them badly, if they put up a fight. I'm not thinking about shattering the skulls of pets. They are chickens, they are nothing. I am letting her off, that's the main thing. She tells me not to.

We go back to the living room and I become morose. I am Satan in defeat. I am not guiding things toward my desired goal. Things are just rolling on. Sharon picks up a broom and says to fence, giving me another one. I participate halfheartedly, then stop. She asks me what I want to do.

It isn't over quickly. I have to talk the articles of clothing off her, and then we come together, and we both are still partially clothed. My leg is on and she asks that I not take it off. It is awkward. The sex isn't complete and is not orgasmic and she comes away frustrated and angry. She sees it as a sign that she has made a mistake, that she has sold out a boyfriend she loves. It's the kind of problem that stymies her. She says that I am a test of faith to her.

It is dark outside and in the cab I realize it's been eight hours since I entered her apartment. She asks if I mind dropping her off at her boyfriend's. I agree, being too happy at the moment with what had occurred to argue.

I go home. Not able to keep track of my funds, there is no food in the house and I have no money. There are no canned goods. No dry goods. No food in the refrigerator and I am ravenous. There is no petty cash downstairs in the office and there is only one counselor on, so she couldn't leave the office to pick up something if there had been petty cash. I am sitting in the living room where all of my belongings have migrated out into the open but none of them is edible. I need someone to rescue me. I hardly eat in the manic but to compensate there are times when I become so hungry I overeat, oversized meals that I store like a camel until the next feeding. The food always tastes good because I have starved myself so long. Now I am in the hunger phase, and I have nothing to reach out to.

I'm hungry.

I'm hungry.

I sit in the shit of paperbacks and hardcovers, hungry, penniless, destitute in my own apartment. This is the dead end. This is the end of a millennium. This is the final test. Christ in the desert. What would I trade for something to eat? Nothing. My datebook lies alongside my knee. I look at it. There are appointments and then the appointments stop. Where the appointments stop, I count three blank dates and write THE FIRST DAY.

# DALKEY ARCHIVE PAPERBACKS

FICTION: AMERICAN

| | |
|---|---:|
| Barnes, Djuna. *Ladies Almanack* | 9.95 |
| Barnes, Djuna. *Ryder* | 11.95 |
| Barth, John. *LETTERS* | 14.95 |
| Barth, John. *Sabbatical* | 12.95 |
| Charyn, Jerome. *The Tar Baby* | 10.95 |
| Coover, Robert. *A Night at the Movies* | 9.95 |
| Crawford, Stanley. *Some Instructions* | 11.95 |
| Daitch, Susan. *Storytown* | 12.95 |
| Dowell, Coleman. *Island People* | 12.95 |
| Dowell, Coleman. *Too Much Flesh and Jabez* | 9.95 |
| Ducornet, Rikki. *The Fountains of Neptune* | 10.95 |
| Ducornet, Rikki. *The Jade Cabinet* | 9.95 |
| Ducornet, Rikki. *Phosphor in Dreamland* | 12.95 |
| Ducornet, Rikki. *The Stain* | 11.95 |
| Eastlake, William. *Lyric of the Circle Heart* | 14.95 |
| Fairbanks, Lauren. *Sister Carrie* | 10.95 |
| Gass, William H. *Willie Masters' Lonesome Wife* | 9.95 |
| Gordon, Karen Elizabeth. *The Red Shoes* | 12.95 |
| Kuryluk, Ewa. *Century 21* | 12.95 |
| Markson, David. *Reader's Block* | 12.95 |
| Markson, David. *Springer's Progress* | 9.95 |
| Markson, David. *Wittgenstein's Mistress* | 11.95 |
| Maso, Carole. *AVA* | 12.95 |
| McElroy, Joseph. *Women and Men* | 15.95 |
| Merrill, James. *The (Diblos) Notebook* | 9.95 |
| Nolledo, Wilfrido D. *But for the Lovers* | 12.95 |
| Seese, June Akers. *Is This What Other Women Feel Too?* | 9.95 |
| Seese, June Akers. *What Waiting Really Means* | 7.95 |
| Sorrentino, Gilbert. *Aberration of Starlight* | 9.95 |
| Sorrentino, Gilbert. *Imaginative Qualities of Actual Things* | 11.95 |
| Sorrentino, Gilbert. *Mulligan Stew* | 13.95 |
| Sorrentino, Gilbert. *Splendide-Hôtel* | 5.95 |
| Sorrentino, Gilbert. *Steelwork* | 9.95 |
| Sorrentino, Gilbert. *Under the Shadow* | 9.95 |
| Stein, Gertrude. *The Making of Americans* | 16.95 |
| Stein, Gertrude. *A Novel of Thank You* | 9.95 |
| Stephens, Michael. *Season at Coole* | 7.95 |
| Woolf, Douglas. *Wall to Wall* | 7.95 |
| Young, Marguerite. *Miss MacIntosh, My Darling* 2-vol. set, | 30.00 |
| Zukofsky, Louis. *Collected Fiction* | 9.95 |
| Zwiren, Scott. *God Head* | 10.95 |

For a complete catalog of our titles, write to Dalkey Archive Press,
Illinois State University, Campus Box 4241, Normal, IL 61790-4241,
fax (309) 438-7422, or visit the Dalkey Archive Press website at
http://www.cas.ilstu.edu/english/dalkey/dalkey.html